NOTHING GOOD HAPPENS AFTER MIDNIGHT

A MIDNIGHT MADNESS NIGHTCREATURE NOVEL
BOOK ONE

LORI HANDELAND

FACING MY GREATEST FEAR

*L*unar Lake, Wisconsin—Spring, 2022

When the phone rings in the middle of the night, everything changes.

Mother always said: *Nothing good happens after midnight.* I'd found in my forty-one years on this earth, in that at least, Mom had been right.

I sat up so fast I jiggled the mattress. I froze, my gaze shifting to, then away from the empty side of the bed. I still hadn't gotten used to Patrick not being there. Would I ever?

The shrill slice of sound continued to cut through the oh so silent night. I only had one ringtone left on my allowed calls after that indelible hour of midnight, and this was it. My heart rate increased from *WTF?* to *OMG!*

"Jenna?"

"Sorry, Mrs. Sullivan. It's Cammy."

I searched my memory for the identity of Cammy, feeling slow, stupid despite the far too rapid rate of my heart.

Spring, same time two years ago, my OB had diagnosed the reason for my newly sluggish brain and sudden ability to fry eggs atop my head as premature menopause.

Look at it this way, you won't have to worry about getting pregnant for very much longer.

Not that I had for decades. However, having my body betray me like that—basically saying I was old, when I never really got to be young—had stung. It still did.

Cammy's tentative voice brought me back to the right now. "I'm Jenna's roommate."

My skin prickled with heat and a fine sheen of sweat started up at my hairline. "What's wrong?"

"Jenna hasn't been here since Tuesday."

Here being the University of Wisconsin. I'd been so proud when Jenna had decided to go to UW like me. Or like the me I could have been, would have been if not for her.

"Tuesday," I repeated. "But it's . . ."

Come on, brain, don't fail me now!

Thursday! I thought at the same time Cammy said, "Thursday."

For an instant, I was near ecstatic to have concluded something at the same speed as a millennial. Then I did the math, never my strong suit even before all the brain-fart BS. "That's two days, and you're just calling me now?"

"Sometimes she pulls an all-nighter. Stays at the library or goes to a study group. But she lets me know. I didn't really worry until I called her phone, and it was . . ."

My skin did that prickle again. Jenna's phone was in Cammy's hand, obviously, since she was talking to me on it. That I hadn't asked *why* earlier put another notch in my losin' it belt.

"Her phone was in her backpack," Cammy continued. "In her room, along with her laptop and her books."

Cammy paused, waiting for me to fill in the blanks. Jenna probably wouldn't be studying without her backpack, and the notes and books and computer within. But even if she'd grabbed a few things and left the rest, she never would have left her cell phone. I didn't think it had been out of her sight—more accu-

2

rately, out of her hand—since I'd handed it to her when she was ten.

"In Lunar Lake, anywhere can be reached from anywhere in a handful of minutes," Patrick had argued. "Even if she falls off her bike and breaks her leg, someone's gonna be at her side quicker than she can make a call. She's safer than safe, like every other kid in town. What are you worried about?"

When I lifted my eyebrows, he'd blinked, said, "Oh," and that had been the last Patrick had said about that. He knew why I was the way I was better than anyone. It was one of the reasons I'd married him.

I'd devoted my life to raising Jenna. She was everything. The *only* thing. When she'd gone to college, I'd been proud but also terrified. This exact scenario—a midnight phone call, a missing child—played through my mind far too often. Sadly, what I should do about it had never played through as well.

"Hello?" Cammy's worried voice broke into my thoughts. She probably thought I'd fainted. Or stroked out. I was tempted.

But all Jenna had was me now, and all I had was her. If that meant facing my greatest fear again, I'd face it. What choice did I have?

She was my baby.

An hour later, I stood in the living room of the apartment Jenna shared with Cammy typing a third, followed by a fourth combination of letters and numbers into Jenna's laptop, but the thing was pass-coded beyond any code either I or Cammy could think of. The one on her phone, the same random collection of numbers Jenna had used and apparently shared with Cammy had not been duplicated on her computer.

"I filled out the missing student report online," Cammy said. "Then talked to the Dean of Students rep when he came by."

"And then?" I clutched the phone so tightly my hand hurt.

"They checked to see if she'd shown up in any of her classes,

LORI HANDELAND

but she"—Cammy's lips trembled—"hadn't. She also bagged a
test, and . . . well . . . you know."

Jenna would never miss a test. She barely missed a class. She'd
wanted to go into veterinary medicine since she was eight and I
accidentally hit a kamikaze squirrel with my mom van. She'd
insisted on taking the thing to the clinic. Five hundred dollars
and two weeks later, the little rodent ran off. I swear it was
laughing.

After that, she'd stopped asking for a pet. Didn't need one as
there were always several somethings being nursed back to tip-
top animal health in our garage.

"Mrs. Sullivan?" Cammy stared at me, worried.

As I couldn't quite remember where we'd been when I floated
off, I smiled as if I hadn't. "Please, go on." Must have been the
right thing to say—score!—because she did.

"The rep from the Dean called the UW–Madison Police
Department. They'd like you to stop by."

"All right. I appreciate you looking out for her."

"She'd have done—" Cammy winced and looked down. "I
mean she *would do* the same for me."

Next thing I knew, I was walking into the building that
housed the UW police. The instant I gave my name to the
desk jockey, two campus cops—one with salt-and-pepper
hair cut bowl-style and a second with dark locks perched
atop an impossibly long face—materialized as if they'd been
hovering just out of sight. Despite the name tags reading
Kowalsky and *Catalano*, my mind had already tagged them
Ernie and Bert. They were both armed, which surprised me
until I considered the commonality of active shooters these
days.

Another tune in the *can't sleep* hit parade that had run through
my head since Jenna climbed into her silver Jetta and motored
southwest-ish for her freshman year.

"I'm afraid no one's seen her," Bert said.

"No one?" I lifted my chin, tilted my head. "On a campus of nearly forty-five thousand?"

"You'd think there would be safety in numbers."

I *had* thought that. Silly me.

"But more students only make a muddle." Ernie spread his hands, a shrug without shoulders.

A muddle? How old *was* this guy?

"We've posted her picture, sent out an alert. So far no responses, but we need to give it some time." Bert inched toward the door. "We have your contact info, and we'll be in touch."

I dug in my toes, both literally inside my favorite black All Birds and figurately with my next words. "Shouldn't you be more concerned?"

"Missing students usually turn up. We haven't lost one since . . ." Bert glanced at Ernie who actually shrugged this time, with his shoulders and everything.

"We've never lost one on my watch."

I wasn't sure I believed that.

"You know who my husband is?"

"Was." Bert set his hand on the door.

I hid my wince with a nod. "Was."

"Of course."

"Then shouldn't you, shouldn't everyone be more alarmed about his missing"—I swallowed—"daughter?"

"It's doubtful anyone kidnapped the child of a dead senator if that's what you're worried about."

Well, shit, *now* I was. I wanted to shout, "Call the FBI!" Maybe I would.

I hadn't turned over Jenna's phone or her computer, and suddenly . . . I didn't want to. Would the university police have the ability to open a password-protected laptop? Could they obtain emails from the server? What about matching names to the even half dozen phone numbers in her recent call list labeled *unavailable*? Sure, I could call one, but I doubted they'd give out their name and location to some stranger who randomly asked for it.

Would the UW police have the connections to get those jobs done?

I suddenly missed Patrick with a desperation that dizzied me. He'd been so capable, so calm. The gap in my life he had filled . . . I didn't think I'd ever fill it again.

I suddenly knew who to call, and I dialed on my way out the door.

"Sarah! You're up early." My late husband's assistant—a beautiful young man with ridiculously long, dark lashes and very shiny teeth—answered on the first ring.

Sometimes, when Frankie had smiled, Patrick would hold up a hand in front of his eyes. "Switch them off!" he'd say, then he and Frankie would laugh. Patrick could make anyone laugh, including me, and I wasn't an easy sell.

Frankie now worked for Gina Garofolo, the congresswoman running for Patrick's senate seat, and according to him, she was a prima drama with a touch of diva on top, so I got down to business.

"Jenna's missing."

"What do you need?"

Frankie never wasted time. Patrick had loved that about him, among other things.

"I have her laptop, but it's password protected, and I can't . . ." I paused to swallow; it wasn't as easy as it had been yesterday. "I can't get in. I've tried all the combos I could think of."

Not figuring out her code . . . it bothered me. Once I would have known it instantly.

Mothers and daughters. It was complicated. We had been close, then Jenna had gone off to college and suddenly we weren't. I didn't know why.

Patrick had given me the "if you love someone set them free" speech. But Jenna hadn't come back; she'd only slid farther away, and no matter how hard I'd tried to find out what I'd done, or maybe not done, I'd never been able to. But she'd had Patrick, and I'd been glad. Jenna needed someone.

However, Patrick was a little too dead to be of any help.

I choked on a laugh-sob. What was *wrong* with me? Besides everything.

Frankie swiftly posed pertinent questions: How long had she been gone? What had been done so far? Who had done it?

"All right," he said. "That's good."

"Is it? The university police don't seem too worked up." Of course, in comparison to me, who would be? "I should go to the locals."

"The UW–Madison Police *are* the locals. They're a full-service department, and they know what they're doing. I promise."

As I trusted Frankie more than almost anyone alive, I contemplated what Jenna had left behind. "Then I should give the officers her phone and—"

"Hell no! I don't care if they're Olivia Benson crossed with Harry Bosch and Hercule Poirot"—Frankie was a bit of a mystery, thriller, crime buff—"they still wouldn't be good enough to investigate anything that has to do with Patrick Sullivan's daughter. Leave this with me."

"I'll bring them to your office."

"Hold off on that a minute. I'm going to make a few calls."

After that I sat in my SUV, stared out the windshield, and tried hard not to have a meltdown. Should I stay here? Should I go . . . where?

I decided eating something, even though I wanted nothing, was a good idea. It was still early, but the Golden Arches were lit, so I drove through, ordered . . . I had no idea what until I opened the bag. A Mc-egg with Mc . . . sausage? I set it aside and picked up the large, piping hot Mc-coffee, nearly dropping it into my Mc-lap when my phone rang.

"Frankie." *Hello* had gone the way of pre–caller ID telephones —into a landfill somewhere.

"I have a call in regarding Jenna's phone log and emails. I also got permission to see the campus security footage."

"How'd you do that so fast?"

"Sarah, please."

The *don't insult me* was left as unsaid as *hello.*

"Where should I meet you?"

Frankie texted the address.

When I arrived, he was leaning against his ridiculous car. Sure, a convertible was sexy—when it wasn't twenty-eight below and your 1957 peacock-blue Ford Fairlane didn't leak wind like a badly caulked attic window.

But Frankie loved that car; it fit his image. Frankie dressed like Gene Kelly, looked like him a bit, even danced like Gene too. Smooth.

I tossed my sweater over the laptop, then stuffed Jenna's phone into the pocket of my brand-new jeans. Since the advent of premature menopause, I'd had to replace all of my pants in a larger size. I was still pissed off.

Frankie took both of my hands and squeezed. "How are you doing?"

I lifted my shoulders. Not well but admitting it would only make me less so.

Frankie's eyes, which matched the car, softened, then he kissed my cheek. He was going to make some guy a fantastic husband one day.

Inside, the tech had the footage keyed up. He pressed *go* and backed off as Jenna emerged from the veterinary diagnostic lab.

"Weird."

"Why?" Frankie's gaze remained riveted, like mine, to the screen.

"She's been accepted into the veterinary program for next fall, but she's still an undergrad, so I'm not sure why she's there."

The lab—well, all the vet school buildings as far as I knew—was pretty far from the campus proper.

"Maybe she had to drop off papers, choose her classes, meet with her adviser," I murmured.

Frankie tapped the time stamp.

2:00 a.m.

My gaze caught on a line of shadows that twirled and fluttered, clinging low to the buildings, keeping pace with Jenna. I blinked, squinted, and they almost realigned into—

"Regardless of if she should have been there," Frankie said, "she *was* there." Silence pulsed for a single beat before, in typical Frankie fashion, he moved on. "I have someone trying to get names for the numbers in her call log that don't have contact info. But her phone was turned off until this morning when it pinged first at her place and then at . . ." He tapped a bit on his screen, then wrinkled his nose. "McDonalds?"

Frankie was a vegetarian.

"She's headed in the direction of her apartment when she leaves the range of this camera." Frankie turned to the tech. "We need to see the footage from the next camera in this direction."

I'd forgotten the man was still in the room.

"She isn't on it."

Dizziness washed over me. I should have eaten the damn Mc-sandwich.

"Then key up the next one," Frankie ordered. "And the one after that, in every direction, all the way to her apartment."

The tech shook his head. "I checked those too."

I'd been prepping for the news that some greasy, grimy, great, hulking brute had dragged my daughter out of camera range by her hair. Or a child asked her to help search for his lost puppy—at 2:00 a.m. near the violent psych ward. Maybe a clown with a red balloon had lured her into a sewer.

I really needed to stop reading Stephen King.

"We wanna see them anyway," Frankie said.

The tech performed his tech-y magic. I watched, hoping, praying, begging that one of those shadows that seemed to flitter and flutter here, there, everywhere, would reshape into a real live girl.

My real live girl.

Except the shadows were gone and so was Jenna. She walked off the frame at the lab, and she never walked into another one.

"How could she be . . .?" I waved my hand at the footage, still focused on the front of the deserted lab. "And then . . .?" I couldn't form a complete thought in my head and make it come out of my mouth.

Frankie thanked the man.

"Yes, thank you," I echoed.

A complete sentence. Yay me.

Frankie took my arm and didn't let go until I was behind the wheel. "You gonna be okay to drive?"

The weight that had descended on my chest in the middle of the night began to thrum, to ache. "Where is she, Frankie?"

He produced a bottle of water from somewhere and pressed it into my hands. "Drink. I'll make a call. I got a guy."

Awesome-Frankie always had a guy.

I drank; it helped. By the time I finished, Frankie had too. "My guy is sending someone who can help."

"FBI?" I got so excited the letters came out high and fast. In every book I'd ever read, every movie, every TV show, the FBI fixed everything.

Frankie made an affirmative noise, followed by "Hold on," as his phone began to ring. He scowled at the caller ID. "I'll just be . . ." He held up one finger before moving a few feet away to take the call.

I wasn't sure how long his call lasted—time had gone funky—but when he said my name, I started so violently he patted my arm.

"I've been assured that the man they're sending is the best at this kind of thing."

"What kind of thing?"

"When people . . ." His voice drifted off as he tried to come up with a better way to say what we both already knew. But there wasn't.

"He's the best at finding people who vanish without a trace," I said.

Frankie's forehead crinkled with concern. "Are you—"

"Yes. Fine. Great. Thanks." I even sounded *fine*, though not *great*. But I could tell Frankie needed to go, probably to deal with whatever crisis had just been related to him by phone.

"He'll meet you in Lunar Lake."

"But . . . shouldn't I stay here?"

"No need." Frankie began to walk backward. "Call me after you talk to him." He jogged the remaining distance to his car with the energy of a thirty-something and was gone before I realized he hadn't told me the man's name. Then again, how many guys who were the best at finding the missing were gonna come knocking on my door in Lunar Lake?

SUNSHINE ON A CLOUDY DAY

*T*he love of my life shook the can of paint and began to tag the huge, flat-topped rock where we'd once shared our very first kiss.

"Yellow because . . ." *He contemplated his work, lifted and lowered one shoulder.* "You know."

The words he'd said to me shortly after we'd met—whenever I look at you, all I see is sunshine on a cloudy day—*I never got tired of them. Sometimes he'd whistle the tune of the last five words, then kiss my hair.*

What eighteen-year-old girl could resist that?

The waves on Lunar Lake slapped and receded, slapped and receded against the rocks below.

Both the town and the lake were dubbed Lunar Lake—creative the town fathers were not. Locals just referred to the body of water as "the lake."

"Whaddya think?"

I tugged my sweater tight against the October chill. The day had been warm, but at night, on the lake, not so much.

He'd painted our initials with a plus sign in between. They seemed lonely on that massive rock. They needed . . .

"One more thing." I held out my hand, and after almost bobbling the paint can into the water, he gave it to me, then he smiled.

That smile. Oh my God. He always insisted that I was the light in his darkness. But to me, he was the promise of dawn pushing against the night, the hope in tomorrow. I wanted him to smile at me like that—

FOREVER

I sprayed the single word beneath our initials, then encased everything with a heart.

He tucked the paint can into the pocket of his battered jean jacket before he pulled me gently into his arms. "Perfect."

I inched my icy hands beneath his shirt. Since he was tall and I was not, his shoulders—narrow as they were—blocked the breeze. He kissed me, and my fingers tightened. His skin was so warm, his belly so flat; I chased the muscles that fluttered there with my thumbs. The scent of Ivory soap caressed my face. When he lifted his mouth, I nearly dragged it back.

"There's nowhere on earth I'd rather be." He laid his cheek on the crown of my head, and I was lost.

My gaze caught on another rock, another tag, another heart—faded, unreadable, it had almost disappeared. Had their love faded and disappeared too?

"Promise me nothing will ever keep us apart."

In the distance, something howled, or maybe it was only the wind that rippled the surface of the lake and made the reflection of the moon dance; it stirred against my temple along with his whisper. "Nothing. Ever."

"Sarah?"

I blinked as the sun sparked off the water, the trees that lined the opposite shore no longer a riot of autumn color but every shade of green. Spring not fall. Warm not cold. Sun not moon. I spun, slipped, would have fallen in, but someone caught me.

The years and the elements had etched their names on his face, but he was handsome in the way that older men could be, that older women could not, with their hair silvered and their eyes surrounded by crow's feet. The sun-warmed shade of his skin caused his gray eyes to flash like steel.

"You okay?" The fingers around my arm, my back were strong, and he pulled me closer when I didn't answer.

Couldn't answer because my body responded as it hadn't in a very, very long time. He was tall, with oceans of lean, hard muscle, instead of tall and still sweetly clumsy with it, but the same scent of Ivory soap tickled my nose. Did anyone use Ivory soap these days? Which made me wonder if the scent was from him, whoever he was, or just floating in on my memories of—?

I stepped away, and he let me go. My treacherous body continued to tingle in places it hadn't. Weird things happened when you didn't have sex for decades.

"I didn't mean to scare you." He jumped from the rock and lifted a hand to help me down.

I folded my arms and stayed right where I was. Strangers in Lunar Lake were either someone else's family, journalists after info on Patrick, or . . . strangers. I didn't like any of them.

"I'm Ash." His arm fell to his side. "Didn't Frankie—?"

"Frankie sent you?" I stepped forward, wobbled, and he offered his hand again.

"He did."

This time I let him help me. I wasn't stupid. If I fell and cracked my head, who was going to make sure Jenna was found?

As soon as my feet hit the ground, I let him go. His warmth, his smell—definitely him—well, everything about him made me twitchy. "You're FBI?"

He lifted his gaze to a sky that had gone the shade of his eyes. "Special task force."

That made me nervous, even before he added a single word that caused my eye to twitch.

"Trafficking."

I wobbled again. Jesus, I really needed to eat something. "You think Jenna . . . she . . . Wait! This is *Wisconsin*."

"Doesn't matter. Human trafficking, *sex* trafficking . . ."

My eye twitched faster.

"Happens everywhere."

"Fandamntastic," I muttered, doing my utmost to keep the flare of anger in place so that the desire to shriek, then panic stayed below. None of those would do Jenna any good. "The FBI has a task force on human trafficking?" I could not get the word *sex* to come out of my mouth, but I wanted to keep him talking, needed to.

"Shouldn't someone?" he asked. "Since the White-Slave Traffic Act of 1910—"

"They really called it that?" Years as a senator's wife had made me, if not completely woke, at least trying very hard to awake.

"Nineteen ten," he said slowly. "It became the Mann Act, not sure when, and yeah, they used it for all sorts of racist shit, but at its heart, the act made it illegal to transport females across state lines for immoral purposes. They've broadened and reshaped it, but it's still a federal offense so . . ."

"We don't know if she's been taken at all, let alone across state lines."

"Frankie gave me a rundown." He spread his big, hard, capable hands. "But why don't you start from the beginning."

I dragged my gaze from those hands with more difficulty than there should have been considering our conversation. *Focus, Sarah!*

I began at the beginning. Saying it out loud hurt—my chest, my stomach, my everything. My life had ended once, then had begun again with her.

"There's no one she'd leave with?" he asked. "Nowhere she'd go?"

"Not without telling me and . . . the security tape. She just . . ." I fluttered my fingers up and away. "How does that happen?"

"Not sure. I've got someone looking at that footage."

"The shadows—" I paused when he shot me a quick, sharp glance.

"What shadows?"

Had those shadows been a figment of my panicked, menopausal brain? Probably. But what if they weren't?

"I saw shadows slinking along the buildings, keeping pace with Jenna. When she disappeared, so did they. They seemed like more than shadows."

"In what way?"

I shut my eyes, tried to snatch that wispy bit of something from the nothing, and got . . . nothing.

"They weren't like any shadows I'd seen before."

"The film may be defective," Ash said. "But we'll check. Anything else?"

I shook my head.

"All right, even though we aren't sure what happened, at this point we'll assume . . . uh . . . well . . ."

"The worst?"

"Sorry, but I've found that gets results."

As results were what I wanted, needed, *had* to have . . .

"What next?" I asked.

"I'm going to follow up on a lead tonight, then I'll be in touch."

My heart began to beat more quickly. "What type of lead?"

"The kind that, I hope, leads to something."

I stared at him a moment, trying to decide whether he was being a smart-ass or just a government employee. In my experience, the latter usually became the former pretty quickly. However, his expression told me nothing.

"I have your number." He backed away, glancing at his watch. "If I find any girls—"

"Girls?" I tried to wrap my mind around the plural but couldn't. My brain repeated *Wisconsin* like a mantra. Like most mantras, it was BS.

"They don't usually put together a task force for just one." He sighed. "Sarah. Sorry, Mrs. Sullivan—"

"Sarah's fine."

He'd already used the name at least once, maybe more than that when I'd been standing on the rock, lost in my past. If he'd tried Mrs. Sullivan, which I'd heard called out by reporters whenever the senator and I had appeared at any function, I'd have ignored him the same as I'd learned to ignore them.

Man, I'd hated the spotlight, but I'd known what Patrick wanted in life when I married him. It was only fair that I stand at his side with a smile after all he'd done for me. He'd been my best friend longer than he'd been my husband and—

"Sarah?"

Sheesh. This wandering brain thing was getting old. Like me.

"Yes. Sorry. Um . . ." What had we been talking about? I said my new favorite phrase, one that often helped me figure out what I'd missed. "Go on."

"Great." He loped away with a lift of his hand.

"Epic fail," I murmured.

He'd seemed off, but what did I know? I'd never met an FBI guy outside of TV. You'd think, being a senator's wife, I would have but no. I stood at Patrick's side when he needed me, and when he didn't, I was here. Lunar Lake was where I'd wanted to be. And the only ones who knew why were Patrick and me.

Make that me.

Our home was the closest one to the lake, and I was glad. If I'd had to walk through town, I'd have had to field question upon question, nosiness couched in concern.

I jaywalked across Lakeview Drive and up the front walk. The house we'd moved into after we married had been in Patrick's family for over a century.

I'd spent what time I didn't with Jenna on the house. Our three-story Victorian had been featured in *Architectural Digest*.

Patrick had been so proud. I was happy to have done something for him. I had done precious little, and I regretted it.

As I stepped onto the refurbished parquet foyer, our final family photo drew my gaze. Jenna had been home for the summer, so had Patrick, and he'd hired a portrait photographer to come to the house.

"You always say you're never in the pictures."

"I do not always say that." In my opinion, I was in far too many pictures.

Mrs. Sullivan! Mrs. Sullivan!

"You know what I mean." Patrick had seemed sad—he knew how much I hated that stuff—and I'd taken his hand, echoing the promise I'd made so many years before.

"I do."

The photographer had snapped a picture, right then, of the two of us. I kept it on the bedside table. But the one that occupied center stage on the dark wood mantle above the marble sitting room fireplace showed the three of us on the porch swing—Jenna in the middle, Patrick's arm along the back. She leaned into him, laughing. I was separate, a little distant, but their bond had made me happy, had made me smile.

The breeze fluttered our hair. Mine, which no longer shone like sunshine—more like moonglow—had mingled with Jenna's.

Dark. Like her father's.

Five months after that picture was taken, Patrick succumbed to the heart attack I'd told him he was due to have if he didn't lower his stress level.

Should I have given Ash a picture of Jenna? How would he know if he'd found her if he didn't have that?

But the FBI knew everything about everyone, right? *Everyone* knew everything about everyone thanks to the goddamn internet. And if he found a girl—any girl or girls—wouldn't he just rescue them?

I let those questions, that worry, slide away. I had plenty of others.

In the sitting room, I ran my hand along the carved walnut armchair, circa 1860. The ivory brocade showed very little wear. Probably because sitting in it felt like sitting in Hell's waiting room. But it looked so damn good.

For a woman who refuses to wear anything uncomfortable, you have a laissez-faire taste in furniture.

Patrick had despaired of me ever being able to arrive at an event without being styled first. He had been as much of a fashion hound as Frankie. Maybe that's why they'd gotten on so well.

Frankie!

I tapped his name in my Favorites list, and when the call went to voice mail, I was tempted to blurt all of my questions. Instead, I just said, "Call me."

Time, which had crept from the instant I answered Cammy's call, kept on creeping.

I should nap, but back when my world fell apart, napping had beckoned too often. I'd been depressed, among other things. I knew that now, and I didn't want to become again the me I'd been then.

Instead, I changed into my paint-spattered clothes and climbed a narrow staircase to the attic. I'd promised Patrick the day we'd moved in that I'd make this area into an office for him. But life happened, and the office didn't. As the third floor was the only place I hadn't done much with beyond cleaning out the crap, I'd made it my next project. I needed one.

Despite the chilly breeze, I opened the dormer window. I'd gotten high on paint fumes once. It wasn't as fun as it sounded.

Maybe this view was the reason I'd never made the third floor into that office. Every time I'd peered out the beautiful bay windows of our sitting room or the bench seat of our bedroom and seen nothing but rocks and water and trees, I'd wondered if I climbed higher, if I saw farther, maybe I'd see all the way into the past. Then I would climb up here.

As much as I'd like to peer outside now and dream of days gone by, I got to work. Painting soothed me. Time sped when I had a brush in my hand; I forgot everything but the rhythm of the movement.

The quicker I covered a wall the appalling shade of . . . I tilted my head, considered the area I had yet to paint over, and landed on, "stomach lining," the better.

In high school art class, I'd begun naming colors what no paint manufacturer ever would. At first because it made Patrick laugh, but later I continued because sometimes there was only one way to describe something such a gruesome tint of pink.

Only you would see it that way, Sunshine.

I dropped the paintbrush, leaving a splotch of minty freshness on my once-white Keds. I hated when that happened. Both the muff of the brush and the whisper of his voice.

I went to the window again and tried to let the not-so-distant waves, the nearly full moon turning their tips an iridescent silver, lull me back to the self I'd become and not the sad, scared self I'd been. Except I was sadder and more scared now than I'd *ever* been, and the waves weren't doing shit.

I glanced at my phone, hoping to see a missed text, a missed call. I hadn't heard a ring or a ding, hadn't felt a rumble, but that didn't mean there hadn't been one. I'd missed calls before when I was in the zone.

Nothing from Frankie, nothing from Ash, nothing from the police, the university, or Cammy.

Nothing from Jenna.

I shoved the stupid, silent phone back into my pocket.

The wind howled off the lake the way it did sometimes—usually in the dead of winter, across the ice not the waves—and the dogs in town howled back.

A shadow emerged from the trees clustered on the opposite

shore. Not a man, not really—the silhouette was too wide in parts, too hunched in others—but when that shadow hurried along the beach in the direction of town, every hair on my arms lifted, fluttered. I raced down two flights, threw open the front door, would have bolted outside—to do what? Got me—if Ash hadn't been in the way.

"Found her." He pushed past me; whomever he held in his arms—head, face obscured by a blanket—did not move.

A watery sigh, maybe a half-sob escaped, and I tightened my lips, put a stop to that, before I pointed the other toward the ivory damask settee.

I'd hemmed and hawed over that thing. Several thousand dollars for a couch? But a Chippendale or Hepplewhite, which I still coveted in a way that probably wasn't healthy, cost upward of seventy grand. Luckily, I'd drawn the line because the visible feet, legs, hands, and clothes now residing on my once pristine, elegant, useless piece of furniture were filthy.

Where had she been? Was she okay? Was she hurt? Why didn't she move? Why didn't she speak?

Ash stepped back. The blanket fell away.

"That isn't her," I said.

SPECTACULAR DISTRACTIONS

*T*he girl was ice pale, her clothes in tatters; she was unconscious. Blond tangles tumbled past her shoulders, the exact shade—*sunshine*—that mine had once been.

"This is who I found. I thought—"

"Just her?"

"You see any others?"

The girl made a sound of distress, and both of our heads whipped in that direction as her eyes opened. They were unfocused and very blue.

Jenna's eyes were brown.

I snatched the picture of the three of us—the one I probably should have given him—off the mantle and tapped Jenna's dark brown strands. Even with the hair, the eyes, this girl looked nothing like me. And except for her hair and her eyes, Jenna did.

Ash took the photo, then frowned. "She said—"

"Jenna! Jenna! Jenna!" the girl announced, then began to laugh like a loon.

Loons really do laugh. They don't sound like lunatics, but she did.

"She said 'Jenna,' so you assumed she was Jenna?"

Ash's eyes narrowed, and his mouth thinned. He was annoyed but so was I.

He shoved his fingers through his hair, and it was then I saw the blood that had dried and the blood that had not, darkening the moldy-moss plaid of his flannel shirt.

"You're hurt," I said.

He lowered his hand. "I'm fine."

He didn't look fine. Neither did the girl, though it was hard to tell under all the dirt.

"Maybe she should go to the hospital," I began, planning to add, "Maybe you should too."

"No!" The girl bolted.

Ash dropped the photo as he caught her around the waist. Gravity sent the frame plummeting to the ground—it was a miracle the glass didn't shatter—then his momentum swung her toward me. He gave a sharp hiss of pain and let her go.

She threw her arms around my neck and laid her head on my shoulder. "No, no, no, no," she whispered.

I rubbed her back and made *mom* noises as I'd done whenever Jenna cried. It had been a while since my daughter voluntarily hugged me, even longer since she cried, but a mom remembers.

She smelled the way Jenna had after she'd volunteered at the animal rescue shelter and been assigned to clean the dog kennels.

"What's your name?" I asked softly.

She didn't answer.

"Can we call your family?"

Still nothin'.

"We should take you—"

"No!" Eyes wild, she bolted again, this time deeper into the house.

Twenty minutes later, she was still MIA.

"Why didn't she hide like this when the traffickers came?" Ash opened another closet door.

"Maybe she did, but they're better at seeking than we are."

"Shouldn't you be better at seeking than this in your own house?"

"Shouldn't you be better at your job?"

He gave me those narrowed gray eyes again. "I found her in a day."

"If only she'd been the one you were looking for. *Where* did you find her?"

"Abandoned warehouses. Other side of the lake."

"Abandoned? I thought that industrial park had been sold." The place had been an eyesore for a while now.

Above our heads, something creaked.

Ash lifted his gaze. "Is that old house noise? Or trafficked girl footstep?"

"I'll find out." I pointed to the floor. "Stay."

His frown deepened the furrow between his eyebrows, but he stayed, or so I thought. When I reached the second floor and glanced back, he stood at the bottom of the stairs.

Had he been watching my ass? No one had in such a long time, I wasn't sure. My ass wasn't bad, but it wasn't what it had once been; it wasn't even *where* it had once been. Neither were my boobs, my stomach, my upper arms, or my chin line.

Welcome to menopause. And why was I thinking these things?

So I didn't think of others.

Like where was *my* girl? And what was being done to her if this poor, nameless kid could barely talk? I needed answers, preferably now, but one step at a time.

I let the world quiet around me, then traced a low hum to Jenna's room, Jenna's closet. I'd checked there before, but I hadn't heard any hum, so I hadn't pulled aside Jenna's floor-length, A-line prom dress, which resembled the sky on the first day of spring, if that sky still held stars that sparkled like diamonds.

Jenna had adored it, and what could I do? Tell her the dress was better suited to my coloring than hers? Some moms would have but not me. I'd had a mom like that and done my best to keep from making the same mistakes, though I'm sure I made new ones.

My fingers had just touched the lace net and satin skirt when I recognized the tune she hummed.

You Are My Sunshine.

I'd sung that song to Jenna every night until she was seven and no longer let me read to her, let alone sing.

I pulled aside the dress to reveal the girl, who stared at Jenna's collection of stuffed wolves—eyes wide, pupils dilated. Terror? Drugs? Or just the darkness of the closet? Though now that I'd let in the light, they should be getting smaller, and they weren't.

She whimpered, pointing to the pile of plush wolves in all shapes, sizes, and shades. At the center perched the black wolf Jenna had found in the front yard the morning after a carnival passed through. When I'd insisted on washing it, she'd stood in the laundry room and stared at the dryer until it was done.

She'd just finished reading *Game of Thrones.* At ten. Not to brag or anything, but Jenna was a bit of genius. Because of her crush on Jon Snow, Patrick had bought her a white wolf, like Ghost in the books and later the show. After that, the wolves became a thing—as evidenced by the pile.

But Jenna always loved that first wolf, the black one, the most. So much so that she began to talk about the large, black beast she saw on the far shore of Lunar Lake. No big deal. Kids imagined things. But when she continued to see it, month after month, year after year, and she was the *only* one who ever saw it . . .

Yeah, she'd earned herself some therapy. Eventually she understood that the wolf was a product of a vivid and wishful imagination. According to the Department of Natural Resources, wolves hadn't been found this far south in a century, and if one *had* drifted away from the pack, someone besides Jenna would have seen it by now.

The wind howled off the lake in that way it did, and the girl's head lifted. The humming stopped. She turned her gaze toward me, toward the light, and her pupils shrank to normal. Thank God, because they'd started to give me the willies almost as much as the humming had.

She scuttled in my direction, never turning her back on the heaping pile of stuffed animals. Her movement struck me as feral, which would be interesting—creepy—even without her reaction to the tower of wolves that weren't real.

"What's wrong?" I asked.

The girl shut her eyes tight. I wanted to grab her and shake her until everything in her head tumbled out of her mouth. But that wouldn't help.

"This one was Jenna's favorite." I touched the black plush ears, worn shiny from use. The white wolf set next to that one toppled over, and the girl flinched.

I waited for her to chant my daughter's name again, followed by that cackling, which had plucked at every hair along my arms and up the back of my neck, but she didn't.

"I'm Sarah." I hoped she'd offer her name, as people do, but again, no response. "Jenna's mom."

She scooted nearer, her bright-blue gaze locked on my own.

"You wanna take a shower?" In the closet, the scent of urine, feces, and wet dog was strong enough to make my eyes water. "You could wear some of . . ." Fearful that my window for using Jenna's name and not hearing it chanted back might have closed, I pointed to the clothes my daughter had left behind. Dresses, skirts, silk blouses.

The girl fingered Jenna's prom dress, and eyebrows paler than mine arched.

"You wanna wear this?"

She smiled. She understood me, even if she wasn't talking.

"Okay." Not appropriate, probably not comfortable, but why not? It wasn't like Jenna would wear again the "froufrou" creation, which was what she'd dubbed the dress her senior year. How quickly times, tastes, and priorities changed.

Weeks away from graduation, nearly a year removed from breaking up with—what the hell had been his name?—she had wrinkled her nose at prom. Instead, she'd picketed the dance, protesting the district's archaic policy on same-sex dates before heading to an overnight party where I was pretty sure she'd had more than a few drinks.

Rite of passage, Patrick had said when she'd come home the next morning and tossed her cookies. *Remember homecoming?*

How could I forget? All those years ago, when the future had seemed so rosy, then suddenly not.

I threw the dress over my arm. Sure, it was borderline crazy for the kid to wear a prom dress, but the sooner she didn't smell like wet, peed-on puppy, the better.

"Come on, sweetie." I beckoned, and she did that weird, scuttling, wild-thing movement. Maybe the prom dress was the least of our worries.

Where had she been? For how long? What had been done to her?

"You'll feel better once you get out of those clothes. Just toss them out the door, okay?"

I led her to Jenna's bathroom, then hovered in the hall until her hand appeared through the crack in the door, the tattered remains of her sweater and jeans clutched in fingernails that looked as if she'd been digging in dirt. Thoughts about *what* she might have been digging—a grave?—I pushed to the back of my brain.

"Come to the kitchen when you're done. I'll fix you something to eat."

She shut the door, locked it, then the shower curtain slid across the bar, the sound both sharp and soothing. The water came on, and I retreated downstairs, making a side trip to toss her clothes into the trash can, then dusting off my hands for good measure. They felt so grimy.

In my kitchen, Ash had made himself at home. Since he balanced a perfectly toasted grilled cheese on a spatula—which smelled like buttery cheddar heaven, comfort food at its best—I didn't care.

"Want one?" he asked.

"Damn right I do, as soon I deal with your . . ." I waved in the general direction of the tattered, bloody remains of his shirt.

"I'm fine," he repeated.

"You're not." I washed my hands, then stepped into the laundry room where I kept my first aid supplies.

Ash followed. When he leaned against the stationary tubs and pulled up his shirt, the space became suddenly too small, too close. I hadn't seen toned male abs in far too long. Hadn't touched any either, and right now, I really wanted to.

"Should I take off my shirt?"

I managed to keep "Yes, please!" from coming out of my mouth. Instead, I shook my head. "This is more than a scratch."

"Is not," came through clenched teeth.

I dabbed antibiotic ointment onto his wound, but the blood just kept washing it away.

"Scratches don't need stitches."

"Neither do I, unless you can do them."

"Got the wrong Sullivan for that."

"You seem pretty good at this."

I shrugged. "Jenna brought home a lot of strays—dogs, cats, birds, kids—most of them needed patching up." Though I always drew the line at stitches. Not only did the act of pulling thread through flesh make me gag but also I liked my face. Stray dogs and cats, even a few of the birds and maybe some of the kids, would become understandably feisty if you poked them with sharp things.

I did my best to cut a strip of gauze wide enough and long

enough to cover the scratches—four of them, close together. They looked a lot like claw marks.

"What's going on, Ash?"

He stared at me with those eerie gray eyes, and I wasn't sure what I saw in them—I was so out of practice.

If I touched the abs I'd been aching to touch, would that cool gray go banked hot coals?

He'd taste like Red Hots candy; he would make my tongue burn. He made *me* burn and yearn in places that hadn't. I couldn't fault myself for being drawn to him.

He began to lower his head; I began to lift myself onto my toes to meet him, then someone gasped, and the lust cleared from his eyes. Had it been there, or had that all been me?

My cheeks flushed, and I whispered, "Not now," to my treacherous hot flash. But there was no stopping it.

His lips quirked. He thought the "not now" had been meant for the girl who stood in the doorway wearing a prom dress without shoes, staring wide-eyed at the bloody shirt, the bloody gauze.

"Press like this." My fingertips grazed his awesome abs, and his hand, blessedly cool, covered mine.

"I have it." His touch, his smile made my chest go tight.

His pocket started to buzz. He retrieved his phone, glanced at it, and the smile disappeared. "I have to take this."

"Of course." I ushered the girl into the kitchen, glancing back as he answered.

"Yes, sir."

The face on the screen was as ancient as my house—icy blue eyes set in a craggy, powder-pale face and framed by a decent head of hair, considering, the shade faded to the yellow-white of the once-golden blond. "Update, *mein Enkel!*"

German? What the hell?

Sure, it was rude, but I listened in. Wouldn't you?

Unfortunately, the rest was in German too—Ash spoke it and

well. Why he spoke it, who that was and what it all had to do with me, with Jenna, with anything were questions for when his call was through.

As I washed my hands again and Ash's blood swirled down the drain, the question he'd never answered—*What's going on?*—pounded in my brain.

I shut off the water; the laundry room had gone silent. When he didn't join me, I left the kid slurping vegetable beef soup and retraced my steps.

Ash was gone as if he'd never been there. No bloody gauze, not a red drip-drop anywhere. My first aid kit had been returned to the proper shelf of the cabinet. If it wasn't for the girl wearing my daughter's prom dress and the red drip-drops in my foyer, I'd have thought I'd lost my mind.

Who was the old guy who spoke German and knew how to FaceTime? Ash's boss? Didn't they have a mandatory retirement age at the FBI?

Had whoever that had been given Ash another lead? If so, why hadn't Ash told me before he'd Houdinied out of there?

Maybe he'd left without a word because I'd almost kissed him —or had he almost kissed me? Seemed a stretch, but what did I know about men like Ash? What did I know about men period?

Had the almost-kiss been a distraction from questions he didn't want to answer? If so, I could almost forgive him. The view of his abs, the look in his eyes, the scent of his skin had all been spectacular distractions.

My phone rang. One glance at caller ID and I stepped into the front hall, keeping an eye on the girl so she didn't rabbit on me too.

"What the hell, Frankie?"

"Did he find her?"

"He did not. He brought me some other girl."

"Brought you . . .?" Frankie echoed. "What?"

"He brought me not-Jenna. The opposite of Jenna. The

antithesis of Jenna." I lowered my voice. "Kid's practically cata-
tonic. Only thing she's adamant on is *not* going to the hospital."

"Let me talk to Ash."

"He's gone."

"Gone where?"

"How would I know? Who is this guy? He—"

"They said he's good."

The *they* stopped me before I could share the phone call, the
old guy, the German.

"Who's they?"

Frankie huffed. "The FBI."

"You really did call them?"

"I said I would."

He sounded insulted, and I guess I couldn't blame him.

"They already knew about other missing girls; they'd
formed a—"

"Task force," I said.

"Right! And Ash is leading it. If he can't find Jenna, no—"
Frankie stopped.

"No one can?" I clenched the phone tighter than tight.

"We'll find her. I promise."

"What should I do with the kid?"

"Put her to bed."

"Jesus, Frankie. Someone's looking for her somewhere. We
need to do something."

"Let Ash figure it out. He's a former marine, a war hero. And
he's been at this job for a long time. I'll be there in the morning."

He hung up before I could ask where he was that he couldn't
get to Lunar Lake until morning. Right then, I wanted to punch
Frankie. I also wanted a glass of wine, but considering I was
babysitting a strange, nonverbal, very weird kid, that was probably not the best idea.

In the kitchen, the girl was nearly asleep in her soup. She
hadn't eaten a lot, mostly the meat from what I could tell. The

grilled cheese—now globby, gooey, coagulated, and cold—remained untouched.

"Come on, sweetie." She lifted her head, groggy as a newborn. "You could use some rest."

She let me tuck her into Jenna's bed, though she would not take off the dress.

"I'm right down the hall." I smoothed her hair. She released a sigh and went lights out in an instant.

I didn't think I'd sleep, but I did. At least until the girl crawled in next to me.

"Shh." She laid her head on my shoulder. "Shh."

My eyes burned. What could I do but tug her close, smooth her hair again, place a kiss on top of her head?

I dozed, unable to fall completely asleep but unable to stay fully awake either. When the girl in my bed thrashed and smacked me in the face, I opened my eyes to a dreary, milky dawn.

NEEDS MUST

J left the girl sleeping, best thing for her, though a doctor's visit was in her future no matter what she wanted.

I'd told Frankie we had to do something. This kid had someone somewhere who was searching for her, crying over her. I was sure of it. So I contacted Patrick's older brother Joe, the present police chief, and I started out by telling him about Jenna.

"You're just calling now?" He said something I didn't quite catch, probably didn't want to. "Be right over."

The line went dead.

Joe resembled Patrick closely enough to make it hard for me to look directly at him without tearing up. Same dishwater hair—though his had not been strategically highlighted the way Patrick's had—same blue eyes, same average height, and same medium build, though at forty-five, Joe had a good start on a belly.

Joe was a jerk. Always had been. I'd asked Patrick why once. His answer?

"Some people are just born that way."

Joe's attitude was all *Longmire*. He'd even added the high-crowned, wide-brimmed hat Walt wore, a bit out of place in small-town Wisconsin, especially during the season where a stocking cap would be advisable, but tell it to Joe.

He had barely removed his hat and stepped through the door when he started badgering me with questions I did my best to answer. Considering his queries, I knew a lot less about the situation than I should.

"Not supposed to work on a relative's case," Joe said. "But I'll put this into ViCAP ASAP."

Joe spoke in acronyms a lot, hazard of the stick up his ass.

"Are you really working on it if you're just inputting information into whatever ViCAP might be?"

"The Violent Criminal Apprehension Program keeps a list of the missing and possible victims of serial crimes. Largest repository of major violent cases in the United States." Joe always sounded like he was rattling off information for a test. But if I let him, sometimes I learned something. "Designed to collect and analyze information about homicides, sexual assaults, missing persons, and other crimes involving unidentified human remains."

"Thanks for the heart failure," I said.

"You should have come to me about Jenna right away. Time is not our friend."

"Frankie sent—"

"Frankie? Really, Sarah? Really?"

Joe had never been a Frankie fan. Despite his ass-i-tude, Joe was capable and honest, he was also so hetero Patrick often said, "He has enough testosterone to give a bull shark a run for his money."

Apparently, bull sharks had the most testosterone on the planet. Patrick knew things like this, no idea why. I missed that about him more than I'd thought I would.

"He called the FBI, and they sent a guy."

"And 'the guy's' name is?"

"Ash."

"First name or last?"

"Um . . ."

"You're killin' me here," Joe muttered. "The agent didn't show any ID?"

Asking for ID. That would have been smart. But why would someone pretend to be FBI, special task force on trafficking, unless they were?

The answer was obvious. They wouldn't.

Would they?

"He . . . uh . . . didn't."

"Sarah!"

In my defense, having my daughter disappear off the face the earth had made me both panicked and desperate. My thought process—which had been murky for a while now—had turned downright foggy.

"The girl might know something, but she's—"

Joe's intense gaze slid in my direction. "What girl?"

That's right. He'd hung up on me before I could tell him.

"The FBI guy . . . he . . . left one here."

Which, come to think of it, wasn't very FBI of him.

"Where is she?"

"Sleeping. I'll . . . um"—I motioned upstairs—"get her."

Of course she was gone; the window gaped open and part of Jenna's dress hung off a snag in the casing, fluttering merrily in the breeze that howled off the lake.

Joe was unamused by the news, even less so by the arrival of Frankie from wherever he had been.

"She was right here." I pointed to the pillows, which clearly showed two head indentations.

"She slept with you?" Joe asked.

"Kid was freaked out."

"No doubt," Frankie murmured.

"I want you to stay out of this." Joe crossed his arms.

"What do you want, Sarah?"

"I want my daughter back yesterday."

Frankie flipped Joe the finger.

"If there's any chance in hell of finding her after you've screwed around this long, I can make that happen quicker than he can, and you know it," Joe said.

"I have resources you haven't even dreamed of, hotshot."

A sob worked its way past my tightened lips, and the two men glanced at me as if they'd forgotten I was there. Happened sometimes in the middle of a pissing contest.

"Did you get the girl's name?"

"I asked; she didn't answer."

"Did she do or say *anything* helpful?"

Jenna's name, loony laughter. Neither was helpful, so I shook my head.

"How about a description for ViCAP?"

"Blond. Blue eyes. Same age and size as Jenna."

Joe frowned. Even I knew that wasn't good considering the anal-retentive nature of serial killers. Did traffickers snatch the same "type" as well?

"What was she wearing?"

"When she got here, a sweater that might once have been pink. As torn as her jeans and filthy as the rest of her."

"And where are those clothes?"

"In a landfill somewhere?" Today had been trash day.

Joe released an aggrieved sigh and peered at the ceiling. He seemed to be counting to ten. I jumped in before he got there.

"They smelled like wet, peed-on puppy." I wrinkled my nose at the memory. "So did she."

"And this?" Joe retrieved the torn section of Jenna's ruined—

"Prom dress. She liked it."

"Long?"

I nodded.

"Shoes?"

I shook my head.

"She climbed through the window in a sparkly prom dress and no shoes." Joe peered outside. "She must have dropped onto the porch roof, then shimmied down a drainpipe. Not easy in that dress but she's young. We had frost last night, so I doubt she got far with bare feet. The question is why'd she run?" He turned to Frankie. "You think your FBI guy might be helpful here?"

"I can make a call."

"You do that." My BIL's chin stuck out almost as far as his chest. If he'd been a turkey, he'd be strutting, feathers spread.

"Joe," I said, trying to unruffle him. "Give Ash a chance. This is what he does."

"What is 'this'?"

"Human trafficking task force."

Joe winced, but at least he didn't say, "We're in Wisconsin."

"We're going to let Ash do his job and help him in any way we can."

"Sarah." Joe's voice held a warning tone I knew far too well. *The family* did not allow outsiders into their business.

Except this business was *my* business, and I was going to do what I should have twenty-odd years ago. I'd wimped out then— torn between gratitude to Patrick and security for me and my unborn child, along with an embarrassing inertia. I had done little during that period but cry, rage, and puke. But I was no longer young, desperate, devastated, or in trouble, and this time I would do whatever I had to do, be whomever I needed to be, infuriate anyone, everyone if it meant getting back the one I loved.

"And if this guy *can't* find her," Joe continued, "if by the time he admits that it's too late to ever find her, then what?"

"Then I guess I'll live with it."

I wasn't sure how. I had barely survived losing Jenna's father. If it hadn't been for his child, I wouldn't have. Losing her was unfathomable. I wasn't *going* to fathom it. And Joe couldn't make me. I mentally stuck out my tongue.

Patrick had trusted Frankie, I trusted him, and if he believed Ash was my best chance of finding Jenna, I did too.

Joe left after promising to keep his trap shut. My in-laws, as good as they'd been to me, were entitled ass pains who'd pull strings, get involved, call the wrong people, and perhaps get Jenna killed. They were also old enough to have the strokes I'd only been dreaming of. I didn't have the time.

"Ash will find her." Frankie stared out the window toward the distant trees as the sound of Joe's cruiser faded. "From what my contact tells me, he's not only a workaholic, but he's obsessed. Ash has seen too much and been able to stop too little."

"Seen too much what?"

"Girls are groomed for . . . things."

I opened my mouth, shut it again. Did I really want to know?

"Sometimes they're used up and spit out, but that doesn't take long. The other option is they become what they need to be, and they're sold. I'm hoping Jenna might be worth more to them than the usual victim, considering her medical background."

"She's a veterinarian. Or will be."

"Doubt anyone involved in human trafficking is gonna care. Needs must, right?" Frankie glanced at his watch. "Gotta run. I'll call later."

He hustled to his Fairlane, top down today. Fifty degrees was pushing it for that, though around here, people wore shorts and flip-flops whenever the temperature climbed above forty-five.

Needs must, right?

After Frankie drove away, I wandered the house, unable to sit, but I couldn't bring myself to paint, even to burn away the edginess tap-dancing on my every nerve. I was no closer to finding Jenna than I'd been yesterday, and it bothered me.

I began to pace—my go-to at times like these. In the past, my pacing had been done in the dark. First with a crying baby, later waiting for the girl who was no longer one, with a few nights in between waiting for, worried about, Patrick. Certainly he was discreet, but there was always a chance that an intrepid reporter might follow him or someone with a camera phone—who didn't have one these days?—and then what?

There'd have been press conferences, interviews, standing by my man, and I would have. Patrick had stood by me. But it would have sucked. A lot.

The day passed quickly. To tell the truth, once I sat down, I think I fell asleep. I *had* spent the night with one ear cocked toward the girl; the night before that I hadn't slept much either.

As darkness fell, I climbed the stairs to the attic and watched moonglow play across the water, undulating, dancing, rippling toward the opposite shore.

When the girl came back, when she beckoned, I wasn't surprised. What else could I do but follow? She was the only lead we had.

Moving swiftly on bare feet, she left the western side of the lake behind and entered the tall stand of trees. The chill didn't seem to bother her. She scooted into, then out of a flash of moonlight that shone through a random gap in the leaf cover, and the torn, shortened skirt of the prom dress revealed fresh, bloody scratches. When you ran through the forest with bare legs, it happened.

I also caught a hint of yellow, of green. Old bruises. Which made me wonder again: Where had she been? For how long? Who had taken her? How had she escaped? What had she seen that had stolen her voice? Had she chosen the prom dress to keep me from seeing her legs?

She moved in a graceful lope that was a far cry from the strange skitter-shuffle of the previous night. Eventually, we spilled out of the trees and into the parking lot of the ghostly industrial park.

Why was she returning to the place Ash had rescued her from?

I wished for my cell phone with all the wish I still had. I'd plugged the thing into the kitchen charger as it was out of juice from carrying it around last night and most of today. I hadn't wanted to let the phone leave my hand, let alone my sight. But when I really needed it . . . didn't have it. A covert agent, I was not.

The girl crept inside the nearest building, and I snuck in after. I hadn't taken more than a few steps before someone grabbed me and clapped their hand over my mouth.

I didn't think, I reacted, jabbing my elbow backward. My arm encountered rock-hard muscle. A grunt of pain preceded the release of my mouth from bondage, and I spun.

Ash. Thank God.

His fingers pressed a non-tattered, non-bloodied shirt the shade of winter tree bark over his wound. I felt bad until he spoke. "What the *hell* are you doing here?"

This from a man who'd snuck out of my house after dropping a traumatized kid in my lap. I'd patched him up! I'd almost kissed him.

"What are *you* doing here?"

"My job. Honestly, Sarah, you're in the way."

"Story of my life. Where's my daughter?"

"Hard to say."

"Hard because you don't want to or hard because you don't know?"

"Take your pick."

He seemed both annoyed and rattled. The annoyed made sense; I didn't belong. I didn't know what I was doing. But shouldn't the leader of an FBI task force be past the point of rattling?

There was no sign of the kid anywhere, though there were

several doorways through which she might have gone. "This place is empty. Why did she bring me here?"

Ash drew me into the shadows where he'd lurked. "It isn't going to be empty for long."

Seconds later a low, savage growl rumbled in the stillness. Ash set his finger to my lips.

"Shhh." His hiss trilled along my nerve endings, along with a second growl.

The moon shone through a skylight as the girl crept out— skitter, shuffle—and the silver beacon sparked off her eyes making them shine as blue as a tropical sky.

"Hey, sweetie," I said, and Ash let out a sharp sigh.

"What is it about 'shh' you don't understand?"

I sidestepped his grasp with a smooth move I didn't have time to pat myself on the back for because the kid snarled and loped straight toward me. She no longer sounded human, which was crazy because what else could she possibly be?

Ash shoved me aside. "In the way, goddamnit!"

My suddenly two left feet stumbled over the buckling concrete. I managed not to fall, but I did take my eyes off the girl, off Ash.

A gun roared, and I cowered, ears ringing, gaze returning to the young woman as fire erupted from the wound. What sort of bullet did that?

An inhuman, unearthly howl rose from the flames as she fell to her hands and knees. Jenna's dress ripped even as it burned.

It was only when Ash ordered, "Stay back," that I realized I'd inched closer. I reached for my phone—nine-one-one in my head— and cursed again my empty pockets, my menopause-boggled brain. Not that there was anything that could be done by anyone now.

The howl died even as she did.

"What did you do?" I whispered—horrified, disgusted, frightened. Ash was nuts or near enough.

"My job," he repeated, and his face . . . I did not want to be the person on the other side of that expression.

"You're not an FBI agent." Not a question, not anymore, but he shook his head anyway, calm, gray gaze pinned on the pyre.

"I search," he said. "I find, then I hunt."

"Human traffickers. But she isn't, she is . . . she *was* . . . their victim. Wasn't she?"

"Until they made her into something else. Something that preys on others, something that now has victims of its own. Or would have if I hadn't been here."

"You're not making sense."

"Come." Ash beckoned, and when I shrank back, he caught my arm, hauled me along. "Look, then you'll see."

I didn't want to peer at a flaming, dead child. Except . . . she wasn't.

I closed my eyes, squeezed hard, then opened them again.

Yep, still a wolf.

THE ONLY GOOD WEREWOLF
IS A DEAD WEREWOLF

*A*sh was crazy. Maybe I was too.

Were we sharing a group delusion? Considering he'd shot a young woman who'd howled like the Wicked Witch of the West—or maybe more like a Dire Wolf—then caught fire as a girl and died as a wolf . . . well, that was pretty delusional. Wasn't it?

"What . . .?" I began. "How? I don't . . . What?"

"Relax. It'll be all right."

"How can this ever be all right?" I'd found my words; I was so proud. "She has a family. A mother, a father. And you just . . . just . . ."

"No." Ash stabbed a finger at the smoldering heap of—

Nope. Not going there.

"*That* no longer had a family. *That* had become a killing machine. Now it won't be." Regret shone in his gaze. "I'm sorry for leaving her with you; I should have done a better job of checking her for a bite. Or at least asked you to."

"What an interesting conversation. 'Please check the pathetic, half-mute, filthy child for a bite mark.'"

I *had* wished I'd done a better job of checking her over, but for normal, less insane examples of what might have happened to someone who'd been trafficked.

"Did you see her bruises?" Thinking about them made me mad. "Those mean she didn't want to become what she did. She was forced into it." Whatever "it" was. "*Trafficked* into it."

"Okay."

I nearly tore out my hair at his indifferent response. "You don't seem to care."

"I do what I do because someone has to."

For an instant, I wondered if he was doing this on his own. While crazy as a shithouse rat.

So where did the lie begin? With Frankie who'd never called the FBI despite saying he had, multiple times. Or with Ash who'd . . . what? Intercepted a call and acted on it? If that were the case, then—

"Where's the guy the FBI was supposed to send?"

"*I'm* the guy. The FBI routes certain cases to me."

"What cases?"

"Right now, any reports of girls going missing in this area."

I got a chill. "How many so far?"

"A helluva lot."

"You still don't seem upset about that."

"Oh, I am. Very."

"But not about . . ." I jabbed my finger at the flaming pile of . . . of . . .

"Being sad about the once-upon-a-time kid now wearing a werewolf suit isn't something I can allow myself to be. I have to move forward, try to save as many as I can before they're turned into—" He jerked his head toward the—

"If I believe this"—I waved at the flames still licking the body —what had been *in* that bullet?—"and I'm not saying I do."

"Sarah—"

I turned my palm toward him in the universal sign for *shut the fuck up.*

"Someone's snatching young women and turning them into werewolves." I had to swallow after that because what was coming from my mouth was ridiculous and yet . . . flaming wolf that had once been a girl. "Why? How? What's the point? Where's the profit?"

"That's a lot for me to go into right now, and I've got places to go, people to see."

"Like hell," I said. "Where's my daughter?"

He cast me another quick glance, as if gauging how close to the edge of reason I was. Damn close, but I was used to hiding it, and I must have done a good job—still had it!—because he answered. Sort of.

"She might be with another pack."

"There are packs?"

"Werewolves behave a lot like real wolves. Packs. Alphas. Betas. But at the basest level, wolves are varmints, vermin, a scourge. Werewolves are worse. They're killers. Always remember, Sarah, never forget: the only good werewolf is a dead werewolf."

"And y-y-you think Jenna's one of them?" Which meant he'd be shooting her at the first opportunity.

"Probably not yet. She's got medical training."

Why did everyone keep saying that?

"She's going to be a *vet*."

He lifted his eyebrows, spread his hands. I heard what I'd said, and inappropriate laughter bubbled. Vet. Werewolves. Get it?

I did what I always did to stop that laughter—coughed, choked, bent over so no one could see my face—though I didn't think Ash would be as disappointed in me over the laughter as Patrick had been. Such behavior had been a biohazard of epic proportion in my unchosen profession.

"You okay?" Ash patted me awkwardly on the back.

I'd have been thankful for his concern if he hadn't been the one who'd caused it. He seemed to think I was throwing up, which wasn't a bad idea considering the smell.

"I'm fine." I waved him off, then stepped back in case I had to run.

"From what I've heard through the grapevine, the werewolves have been getting sick."

Over what grapevine would he hear that? *Looney Tunes Ltd.*?

"The virus has killed all the females."

I guess that answered *why* as well as *what's the point* and *where's the profit*? A three-fer!

"What about this girl?" I lifted my chin to indicate what was no longer a girl, or even a wolf, but a pile of sizzling flesh turning to ash. Using flame-inducing bullets made cleanups a snap.

Was Ash really his name or only what he was called because of . . . My gaze caught on the dwindling gray flecks as they cast across my shoes, then swirled away.

I coughed again, and Ash frowned—part concern, part annoyance. I supposed if I passed out, puked, melted down, had a stroke or a heart attack he'd have to deal with me and not his *places to go, people to see.*

Or perhaps he'd just leave me lying there.

"What *about* this girl?" he asked.

"She's a girl. Female."

He continued to stare at me blankly.

"She didn't die by virus, Ash."

"Ah." He nodded. "I've also heard whispers of a cure."

I guess there had to be. Otherwise, why kidnap girls, change them, traffic them, then sell them if they were only going to get sick and die?

I'd had another question. What had it been? I rifled through my Swiss cheese brain and nearly danced a jig when I remembered.

"Someone has to be searching for this kid. Isn't she in ViCAP?"

Although if she was, wouldn't Joe have found her by now and let me know? Then again, Joe had only a verbal description to go on. No photo, no name, no nothin'.

"I'll handle it."

"How?"

He huffed, impatient. "Sarah, I'm just a guy doing his job. That's all."

Ash wasn't "just" a guy. He was a guy who kept exploding bullets in a gun that turned young women into wolves, then incinerated the remains, which floated away.

If I made a mistake here, my daughter would pay for it, and that was *not* going to happen. I'd figure out later how to get word to someone, anyone, about the dead girl. Right now all I cared about was finding Jenna. No one, nothing mattered but that.

I was a sociopath when it came to my child. Sue me.

"Now what?" I asked.

"Now I take you home and do what I do."

While I really wanted to get home and wash the scent of flaming wolf-kid out of my hair, I wasn't going to let Ash out of my sight. I resigned myself to smelling like human BBQ at least for tonight. Werewolves only come out at night, right?

Hysterical laughter burbled, but a sudden commotion outside put a stop to that. Voices—male, a lot of them—drifted through the jagged glass of the broken window across the room.

Ash's head whipped that way as fast as a gun appeared in his hand. "Stay here." He hurried across the floor.

I flipped his back a double bird and followed. He didn't stay when I told him to, why should I when he told me to?

He crouched to the left of the window, scowling when I took the right. "You get bitten, and I'll shoot you quicker than I shot the last one."

I had no doubt he would. We'd nearly kissed in my laundry room. He'd made me feel things I hadn't in a long time. Still, I'd shoot his ass too if it helped me complete *my* mission—saving

Jenna first, then any other trafficked girl trapped in this horror novel.

Between our building and the next, two groups of men postured, bristled, their eyes squinty and fists tight; the scent of sweat and musk, of hatred and fury clouded the air. I half expected them to start snapping their fingers and singing "The Rumble" from *West Side Story* or maybe "Beat It."

My mother had been an MJ fan since he had his first nose.

"The battle is now." A growl rippled beneath the words of the speaker.

"Victory will soon be ours," a guy on the other side of the invisible dividing line said, his lip lifted in an unattractive snarl. His hair was long, tangled, either dirty blond or blond and very dirty.

"Or ours-s-s-s." The first man who'd spoken drew the word out and into a hiss. His dark hair had been shorn close to his oddly triangular head. If my head were shaped like that, I'd go for the shaggy not the shorn.

Beyond the two speakers, Dirty Blond and Triangle Head, what looked to be a secure, *Star Wars*–epic-style, blast-proof door —very different from the easy-peasy one I'd walked through to get in here—opened. The two groups filed in amid jostling, growling, and shoulder bumping. Men were such boys.

"Stay," Ash said again, and sprinted for the entrance, keeping low even though it seemed like everyone had entered the other warehouse.

The door shut behind them with a hearty *thunk-click*.

Were there stragglers, maybe snipers? No idea, so when I followed, I kept my head low too. Couldn't hurt.

Ash stopped abruptly five feet from the exit, and I slammed into him, nearly falling on my ass.

He grabbed me as I toppled backward and gave me a gentle shake before releasing me. "What don't you understand about 'stay'?"

"Not a dog." I forced the nervous giggle back where it belonged. Brain, throat, stomach? Take your pick.

"Listen, I'd have preferred to take you home before I had to . . ." He waved at the other building. "But I don't have time. The winning pack gets the prizes. Tonight."

"Prizes." A bad feeling crept over me.

"Women. They need them. Haven't you been listening?"

The world I'd entered, the world that lived beneath the one I knew and wanted back so damn bad, was violent, horrifying, frightening to the point of inertia. But inertia was something I could not afford.

"Haven't you?" Why wasn't *he* getting it? "I will do anything to find my daughter. If you think Jenna is in there, or there might be someone who knows where she is, I'm going too."

"These are werewolves, Sarah. They have no mercy; they have no souls. Unless you have value, they will kill you and move on without question, without doubt, without a second thought."

"Without her, what's there to live for anyway?"

A flick of his eyes in my direction was his only answer.

"I need to slip inside while they're distracted by the bout."

"Bout?" I sounded like a parrot, even to my own ears.

"A battle between packs is fought by alphas, to the death. The leaderless pack will be absorbed into the victor's, making it stronger. Everyone in that warehouse will be affected by the outcome."

"And they aren't going to be looking out for you."

"Now you're catching on." Ash lifted the fully automatic rifle that leaned against the wall near the door, along with a Ramboesque bandolier full of, most likely, bullets that went kaboom. He tossed the latter over his head so it fit crosswise as a bandolier should, adjusting it so the pistol at his hip remained unobstructed.

I'd bypassed the weapon, the ammo without a glance when I'd followed the girl into this building. I only recognized the type of rifle because Patrick had been on a committee trying to pass anti–assault rifle legislation, despite blah-blah-blah Second Amendment.

I'd suggested allowing whatever weapons had been common in the late eighteenth century, when the Constitution had been written, and banning the rest. I doubt our forefathers could ever have imagined the sort of firepower Ash carried now. Wouldn't the number of school shootings take a complete nose dive if the asshole with the gun couldn't fire more than three shots per minute because he had to pour powder into the barrel, pop in a ball, use a ramrod, prime it, cock it? I *had* done my homework on this.

Patrick had not taken my suggestion to the committee. He'd thought I was kidding; I was not.

Nevertheless, the rifle Ash held was illegal in the US. Not that the bad guys, whoever they were this week, didn't have some.

"I cannot rescue any girls if I'm worrying about you too. Go. Home. I'll meet you there."

If he was still alive.

He waited for me to agree, and while I hated to lie, couldn't get it out of my mouth, I could nod. I'd been doing it so much lately I felt like a bobblehead affixed to the dashboard of a vintage car.

Ash slipped out the door. I stayed where I was long enough for him to get to where he was going without seeing me slink after. No way in hell was I going home if Jenna might be nearby.

If Ash had understood what I would risk, where I would go, what I would do for my daughter, he never would have left without tying me up.

A peek around the doorjamb revealed him picking the lock. Took him a while but he managed, an impressive feat considering the door. When he opened it, loud rap music blared free. The pulsing beat beneath the lyrics echoed the blood-thumping beat of a heart.

I had no idea who the artist was, how old or new the song. I knew little about rap beyond forbidding Jenna to listen to it, then finding a playlist on her phone with some of the most misogynistic, violent crap I'd ever heard under the false heading of an innocuous country rock band.

Patrick had applauded her ingenuity. I'd grounded her for a month. I didn't care for lies, even though my life and hers were based on them.

Ash stepped inside, and I ran. He wasn't going to let the door slam behind him and draw attention, which meant it closed ever so slowly but still faster than I could run. My legs were short: I was short and not in tip-top shape. My fingers brushed the handle half a second after the door clicked shut.

"Fuckety fuck!"

One happy result of Patrick's death—the only one—was that I could indulge my hobby of curse-word innovation.

Since I could not get in through this entrance, I searched for another. My reward for not being a quitter lay at the rear of the building. A window, too high for me to see into but open so that the headache-inducing *thrum* that had to stir up the ire of both man and wolf poured out.

Several discarded plastic milk crates created a dangerously rickety ladder. As I reached the pinnacle, the now familiar scent of wet, peed-on puppy wafted past. A single peek revealed why—cage after cage, occupied by girl after filthy girl, plus three chained to a wall with iron dog collars sporting spikes like the bulldog's in *Tom & Jerry* cartoons.

I boosted myself over the ledge, did a fancy twirl on my ass that made me quite proud, dangled my legs, and let go.

My feet touched concrete, and I followed my momentum into a crouch. Beyond the doorless entryway—gotta keep an eye on those prizes—the moon shone through a skylight like Batman's beacon, illuminating a circle where two wolves waited. For a second, my still back-in-the-land-of no-werewolves brain—ah, I missed it—insisted there'd been two wolves in the cages in front of me. Like a dog-fighting ring, disgusting yes, but it made more sense than werewolf rumble.

Except every cage was occupied—none by Jenna—and I blinked against the burn of tears. Where was she if not there?

In the ring, the first combatant—a great, black beast, his silky coat shimmering with threads of sapphire—stood impossibly still, his topaz gaze pinned on his prey.

The second paced back and forth, white fur shimmering in a nonexistent breeze; the flicker, flash, flicker of the moon painted incandescent, mother-of-pearl highlights wherever it touched and made his emerald eyes shimmer. Wolf-long legs—once you saw a wolf, you would never, ever mistake it for a dog—stretched his shadow until it melded with that of his opponent's.

Black wolf versus white wolf. How trite could they be?

The Sharks circled one side, the Jets circled the other, a healthy distance between the two. The scents of sweat, musk, animal, and man swirled together to create a violent expectation that hung heavy in the air.

Ash was there—somewhere—but I didn't see him anywhere.

The roar of the crowd, the thrum of the music ceased, the sudden lack of sound causing the silence to pulse. Every eye in the place stared raptly at the exceedingly tall man of indeterminate age. He had to be six-seven if he was an inch, though he might weigh one-ninety on a rainy day. His suit, which probably cost a grand, was the same charcoal shade as his undulating waves of waist-length hair.

His face was downright fugly. I felt bad for thinking so—what did appearance matter?—but the combination of his features did not come together with any sort of symmetry. He resembled a praying mantis, all legs and elbows and buggy eyes.

He strolled the outskirts of the ring; a silvery glow trailed from his fingertips, encasing the rumble in a shimmering circle of fog. When he reached the place where he'd begun, he lifted both hands like a revivalist preacher, and I swear every being in the room held its breath. I did.

Who was he? What was he? Why—

His arms slashed down, and the crowd roared; the music recommenced, and the two animals inside the ring slammed into each other, chests thumping, jaws snapping. Fur flew, blood spattered, fangs flashed. I cringed.

My movement drew the attention of one of the caged girls, then another; awareness of possible salvation rippled from enclosure to enclosure. I swiped any trace of saltwater weakness from my face. I wasn't cut out for this, but that didn't mean I would stop. My daughter might not be there, but if I could get the others out, I would. I reached for the release on the nearest cage and cursed. It was padlocked.

"What did you expect?" the obviously bottle blonde in the nearest enclosure asked, her volume just below a shout.

I glanced behind me. No one had heard us. Sure, the music was loud, but didn't werewolves have batlike hearing? Perhaps they had become immune to the shouts and cries of their prizes. Whatever the reason, it made things easier for me.

The girl in the cage I'd tried to open seemed listless, maybe feverish, certainly close to unconscious; she'd be no help.

"I don't suppose anyone's seen a bolt cutter?" Though I doubted my hands were strong enough to use one.

Bottle Blondie blew air through her lips—a snort without the nose. "There's a key on the wall."

"Well, that's dumb." Both them for leaving it and me for missing it.

"Not like they let us out without a leash or a guard." A redhead with hair so bright it shone through the filth smacked a palm against the cage door.

"This is inhumane," I said.

"They are." The redhead's burst of laughter bordered on hysteria.

I snatched the key as a yip, then a howl lifted toward the skylight. A trail of steam lifted too, followed by the acrid scent of burned hair, and I understood the reason behind the smoky silver circle. If a wolf—for some reason my brain refused to think of them as werewolves quite yet—got too close . . . hiss, yelp, scorch.

Smoke still trailed from the black wolf's haunch; they both dripped blood. Splashes of gruesome crimson streaked the concrete; bubblegum-pink foam flecked their mouths. The black wolf's right ear was missing; the white wolf's eye was.

Still no sign of Ash and it worried me.

I concentrated on my task, and soon after, seven cages swung open; seven girls crept out. I pointed to the window. "Go!"

They didn't have to be told twice. The redhead and Bottle Blondie supported the sick girl, one on each side. I hoped they could boost her to the window, that someone taller than me was willing to be the last one out and capable of pulling herself upward without help.

The cage key didn't fit the lock on the collars, but I found another just out of reach of the nearest girl's fingers. The consideration flashed through my brain that leaving keys in sight, so close and yet so far, was a purposeful mental torture. Same as the bloody welts on the nearest girl's neck, which revealed she'd tried, failed, and tried again to reach that key, was a physical one. She appeared so young, so broken I wanted to hold her, but we needed to move.

"I'm looking for my daughter."

The *snick* of the lock's release would have been followed by the *clangedy-clack* of both her collar and the chains hitting the floor if I hadn't been ready for it and lowered the iron restraints to the ground, slow and easy. Sooner or later, someone out there was gonna hear something in here.

"Jenna?" I continued, and the girl's big blue eyes slid away from mine. I got a very bad feeling. "Jenna Sullivan?"

"I haven't seen her since—" She chewed her lip and continued to stare at the floor.

"Since when?" I clapped my hand on her shoulder, and she winced. I let go as quickly as I'd grabbed on. How could I have forgotten her neck? My only excuse was the panic that made my plea difficult to push past the tightness in my throat. "Tell me. Please."

She inhaled, then blurted words so quick and quiet I had to lean close, ignore the smell. "I'm not sure how long ago it was. Time doesn't have much meaning when you're . . ." Her eyes flicked quickly to, then away from those chains. "She put something on my neck so it wouldn't get infected. Did her best to calm the ones that were losing it." Her lips lifted just a little. "She sang to them. Seemed to help."

That explained the disconcerting rendition of *You Are My Sunshine* from the wolf girl in the closet, but I still didn't know where Jenna was.

"And then?"

"Jenna had a pretty big hissy about the one over there." She lifted her chin to indicate the now empty cage where the feverish girl had been. "So they sent for their alpha."

"Their what?"

"He's like a king. Of werewolves."

I choked on my response to that ridiculousness—hysterical laughter that would sound like the redhead's—but she didn't notice.

"Actually, both groups have one, so more like leader of the pack."

That's when I fell for . . . singsonged through my head and nearly out of my mouth. She was too young to remember it; I would be too if Patrick hadn't loved sixties music.

I released the final two girls. They sprinted for the window where, indeed, the tallest had remained behind to help. Her pale, long, gorgeous hair swayed as she moved, causing a tingle of recognition; however, the connection slipped my mind as connections did lately.

"What did this 'leader of the pack' do?"

"Took one look at Jenna and ordered her dragged out of here. I haven't seen her since."

That didn't sound good.

The girl scooted across the cell and clambered out the window after being boosted by the last, who then beckoned me. "One of them's coming."

I scooted for the window faster than the previous kid had.

The final girl made a stirrup with her hands. "You first."

I hesitated, and she made a sound of exasperation. "You're too short to reach the window without help. I'm not."

She was right. Even using all of my strength—I'd never had much and these days even less—I couldn't make it until the kid gave my ass a mighty push. Before I could lean down to help her, the trafficker, the werewolf, hell . . . the werewolf-trafficker came through the doorway like a bull that had sighted red.

The girl dodged; she ducked, avoiding him easily despite the size of the room. He was huge but he didn't move as fast as she did.

"Flag someone down," I told the last girl who'd made it out and hadn't yet joined the rest sprinting for the cover of the trees. "Call the cops. Hurry!" I launched myself from the window ledge and back into the building.

"Hey!" I shouted as I landed, stumbled, gained my feet.

The guy, silhouetted in the doorway by the slant of the moon, turned. The girl scuttled in my direction, then a burst of automatic gunfire had us both hitting the deck.

Our soon-to-be attacker went up in a ball of fire. He howled in agony and fell onto all fours, changing even as the fire danced.

Ash stepped into the room. "Jesus, Sarah, do you ever stay put?"

I considered giving Ash a finger or two—he hadn't seen my

earlier ones—however, his fury was understandable. I'd ignored every warning; I had disobeyed every order. Both of the behaviors were new to someone who'd spent years following all the rules.

It occurred to me to wonder how Ash had planned to rescue the girls on his own.

I guess if he blasted every werewolf, leaving pile after flaming pile on the concrete floor, he could do whatever he wanted when he finished. Take his sweet time. Lead them through the door together, instead of urging them out the window girl by girl. In my defense, my way *had* worked.

The cessation of the rap music made my ears ring with a phantom *bum-bum-bum*.

Ash spun, spraying gunfire across the first wave of approaching man-wolves. Flames exploded, same as the last, so high, so hot the second wave fell back, snarling, growling.

Those sounds coming from men made me shiver despite the flaring heat.

I hoped that by now the girls had flagged down a passing car, used the driver's cell phone, and the cavalry was on the way. Sure, there were holes in my plan—big, gaping, scary holes filled with werewolves chasing them through the forest, munching on the escapees before Joe and his officers could arrive.

And what would Joe do when the wolves kept coming despite being shot multiple times with lead?

Die, that's what.

I needed to get out of there, warn Joe, the town, the army. Someone. Anyone.

Everyone.

"Go," Ash ordered, just as I had, then sprayed the second wave with bullets.

Suddenly I loved that weapon.

I hurried to the window as the girl stepped from the shadows, rapt gaze not on me but on Ash. Utter joy washed over her face.

She moved closer, and the slant of the moon shone through the only window, causing her hair to gleam first silver, then gold. I remembered where I'd seen that color half a second before she murmured, "Uncle Ash?"

How he heard her above the crackle of flames, the snarls of a third wave, I didn't know. But he glanced at us, freezing just long enough for her to start toward him, then he lifted his rifle and aimed at his niece.

WE'RE THE SHADOWS;
WE'RE THE WIND

I shoved the girl aside, and pain exploded in my arm—scalding, fiery—I thought I might go up in a great ball of fire. That I didn't answered my question about the bullets in Ash's gun. *They* didn't explode, what they were made of caused certain people—werewolves—to go boom. Good to know.

The weapon went silent as fast as it had gone loud, and Ash fell to his knees at my side. The firearm clattered onto the concrete floor. "What is wrong with you?"

"How long you got?"

From the corner of my eye, I saw his niece lift herself into the open window, then slip over the edge and disappear.

Ash tore the shirt from my shoulder.

"Hey! This is my favorite sh—" I glanced down. Said shirt was covered in blood. I knew from the years I'd washed Jenna's clothes after she'd played vet that blood was a bitch to get out, and my favorite shirt was toast.

"Good." Ash pressed his palm to the wound so hard I drew in a breath. "The bullet went straight through the meat of your upper arm."

Let's hear it for the menopausal upper arm jiggle!

"We gotta stop the bleeding." His gaze flicked around the room. As he registered the empty cages, the empty chains, the shadowed but empty corners without his niece, his mouth tightened. "What have you done?"

"Saved the girls. You weren't going to."

"They were all bitten."

"How can you know that?"

"I know how werewolves operate. The girls were here to become part of the problem. My job is to solve problems."

"You're crazy," I muttered, but unease trickled down my spine. *Had* I unleashed werewolves on an unsuspecting world?

The uneasy trickle amplified into dizziness, faintness, and nausea.

"They're going to change." Ash tore a strip off my shirt, wound it around my arm, and yanked.

The room wavered; I fought against the nether land of pain and blood.

"They're going to bite, maybe kill, others."

Seemingly out of nowhere, the Shark, or maybe he was a Jet, saddled with the triangular noggin appeared behind Ash, snatched his rifle off the floor, and banged him on the head.

Ash collapsed into my lap, and I swallowed a moan as he jarred my body. My wound dripped blood into his hair.

With no one, nothing to stop their advance once the flames receded, the third wave crowded through the open doorway. Had any of them gone after the girls?

Counting in my head what I thought I'd seen during the rumble, then subtracting the number I thought had died, plus these, I didn't think so. Then again, there were a lot of *thoughts* in that sentence, and I didn't do math. Add to that my fuzzy vision as several of the approaching men merged, separated, merged, and I had to admit I hadn't a clue.

They grabbed Ash, and I clutched at him with my workable hand, but several others yanked me to my feet. I wobbled as the world whirled, reminding me of how it felt to be drunk—bed spinning, me puking.

"Remember our orders," Triangle Head said. "No harm comes to them. Yet."

"He killed my brother, and he ended the battle before they finished. *She* freed the prizes we were promised." The guy on my left adjusted his package with the hand not holding on to me. "I need a release." His gaze shifted in my direction.

"You wanna deal with our alpha after you've disobeyed an order?"

The guy paled, and his hand dropped from his crotch. I had an instant to hope he never used that hand, or anything else, on me before they dragged me toward the doorless door, and the pressure on my wound made everything go bright red. Then I didn't hope, didn't think, didn't hear, see, or smell for a long time.

I awoke in a damp prison cell, my arm on fire, my shirt cemented to my skin by dried blood. The worst part? I was chained to the wall with one of those demoralizing steel-spiked dog collars. That really pissed me off. I held on to that anger because, somehow, it pushed the terrified beneath.

Ash slumped against my wounded side, his silver-gold hair bisected with rust-colored streaks, same as his pale-pale face. He was so still—too still—and for a minute, I could barely breathe at the thought of being left alone.

My fingers crept to his wrist. He still had a pulse.

Ash sat up as if he'd been goosed, lifting a hand to his head. The manacle scraped his face; the chain attached between it and the wall, just like his other hand, rattled. When his fingers encountered the crack in his head, he winced. When he lowered his hand, fresh blood made his fingertips sparkle in the half light. He stared at the chains as if he couldn't quite figure out what they were.

For the first time in quite a while, I worried about someone else's mind instead of my own. It didn't feel any better; I wasn't worried any less. Ash and I were in this together now, and I needed him sharp, or at least sharper than me.

"What happened?"

I was thrilled he spoke sense. You'd think he'd be loopy, but the man must have the hardest head around.

Before I could answer, voices drifted from beyond the bars where freedom lived.

"Let's hope they've corralled the prizes before they reached Lunar Lake."

Ash gingerly rested his head on my shoulder once more, then closed his eyes. "Shh."

I got the hint. If they thought we were still unconscious, we might hear something useful; my eyes closed too.

"What do we care about Podunk-ville?" a second voice demanded.

"The deaths and disappearances of a good portion, maybe an entire population of even a small town is going to bring more attention, more law enforcement, more guns."

A good portion? The entire population?

That *couldn't* happen because I'd released trafficked girls. I didn't deserve that. Neither did anyone in Lunar Lake, but I'd learned long ago that what we deserved—good or bad—was rarely what happened. Karma was bullshit.

Tears burned my eyes, acid burned my throat, and I swallowed. Now was not the time for puking. Really, when *was* the time?

As if he knew what I was thinking, feeling, Ash inched closer. His presence calmed me. We were probably going to die soon, but at least we wouldn't die alone.

"Without silver bullets, guns are no more a danger to us than sticks in their hands."

Silver bullets. Once upon a time, I'd have figured that out on my own.

"We have to be smart."

"People disappear all the time."

"Maybe so, but there hasn't been a whole town gone missing since those goddamn idiots wiped out Roanoke."

My eyes flicked open. *Roanoke? Seriously?*

Ash twitched his shoulder, and my eyelids snapped closed. But not before I caught a glimpse of a redhead with so many freckles so close together his entire face was the shade of old, flaking dried blood; the second man was the shaggy dirty blond we'd seen outside.

Ash remained tense, ready, waiting. For what? He had no gun, no silver bullets, hell, no silver anything, no backup as far as I knew, and we were chained to a wall on the wrong side of a locked prison door.

"Nobody ever figured out what happened on that island," Dirty Blond said.

Roanoke was an island? Huh. Learned something new every day.

"In 1590, they had no way of figuring anything out. Now there are security cameras everywhere, people recording with cell phones, ring video on their doorbells."

"On film, we're the shadows; we're the wind."

Well, that explained the creepy, slinking shades on the security video. I wasn't crazy! Bonus points.

It did not, however, explain how Jenna had disappeared from the same footage.

"Shadows and wind can't kill, maim, create other shadows and wind."

"So people are gonna jump to werewolf massacre?"

"At the least they'll jump to starving or rabid wolf pack, smart enough to avoid recording devices. That rumor gets around, other hunters will come. A lot of them."

"But we haven't *done* anything."

From Ash came a soft, derisive sound, but the two men did not barrel into the cell and beat the crap out of the guy who had killed so many of their kind. They did not do . . . whatever evil, soulless creatures did to women they'd captured. Instead, their voices became fainter and fainter.

"We haven't done anything *lately*, but Badru's pack certainly has."

A change rippled over Ash at the sound of that name. His breath came faster, the speed reminding me of a Lamaze technique that was supposed to help the pain of childbirth. It hadn't. His head on my shoulder became heavier as if he were losing consciousness; his skin seemed to radiate a sudden heat.

"If we're lucky, they were able to retrieve the prizes before they hit town." The guy with the freckles spoke fast, hope lighting his voice. "No other hunters will come, then Alpha will win the battle, and this will all be over."

One of the alphas' names was Alpha? How was that for a god complex? Couldn't wait to meet the guy. Then again, maybe I could.

Silence descended for several ticks of the clock before Freckles broke it. "What do you think we'll do with the hunter?"

"After he mowed down two-thirds of the pack, I'd like to shoot him in the head and toss him into a ravine."

I winced so hard I had to fold my lips tight to keep the hiss of pain inside when my movement caused Ash's head to slide over my wound.

"What about her? I bet she was hot in her day, but those days are gone."

"Long gone."

Ouch! Was that necessary? Sure, I'd let myself go a bit, but no one who loved me cared. Lately, *I* didn't care. What difference did my appearance make? None, unless I was captured by werewolves and tossed aside because I was no longer hot enough.

"You think Alpha will let her go?"

"No," Dirty Blond said, "I don't."

I had a bad feeling I was gonna join Ash in a ravine. Why hadn't I stayed home?

Jenna. Right. Still hadn't found her. Was Ash wrong in his belief that her minute medical knowledge would be useful enough to keep her human longer than rest? Or had she already been changed and sold?

Would I discover the truth before I met that ravine? Hard to say. The Sharks and the Jets had enough going on that they might not have time to worry about us right now.

"What if she's someone important? Someone that someone else won't stop looking for?"

Once upon a time, someone would have kept looking for me, even though I had not kept looking for him. I'd had a good excuse. The same excuse I had now for never giving up this search as long as I lived.

Our child.

But was there anyone anywhere *anymore* who might keep looking for me?

"Relax. We're safe; we're alive."

"This hunter found us, killed us, so not all safe, not all alive."

"If you don't like what's going on, if you think you could do better, challenge the alpha." Dirty Blond's footsteps receded.

"I know how the pack works." Freckles followed his pal.

A door opened, then clanged shut, and Ash lifted his head. He frowned so hard I worried he was having an aneurysm.

I touched his arm, half expecting him to start violently, having forgotten I was there.

Instead, he turned to me, eyes sharp and aware, though the frown remained. "I don't understand why one pack is trying to contain this. Werewolves kill; they create other werewolves. What's wrong with these guys?"

"If they're so different from the others, maybe you should ask what's right with them. And why."

"There's nothing right about werewolves no matter how much you might want there to be."

I did want that. Wanting that was the only hope I had, considering our chances of rescue seemed slim to none.

"Why do you hate them so much?" I asked.

"What's there to like? At worst, they're crazed, soulless, killing machines. At best, they're crazed, soulless, virus spreaders."

Ash wasn't there because of any gung-ho need to stop a horde or two of those crazed, soulless, virus-spreading, killing machines. At least at the heart of it. At the heart of it was the final girl.

The one he'd tried to kill.

"She called you Uncle Ash."

He flinched.

"Wanna explain that?"

"I do not." He lowered his gaze to his manacled wrists. "But what else I got to do, right?"

I didn't answer since we both knew the only other thing he had to do was die.

Ash continued to stare at his bound hands. "My grandfather returned from World War Two having seen things, having killed things for which there was no explanation. He swore to rid the world of what he'd found there, what he found pretty much everywhere once he knew how to look."

"Werewolves."

"Monsters," Ash said.

"Plural?"

Ash lifted his gaze, met mine, nodded.

My mouth fell open; I had *not* seen that coming, and I probably should have. If there were werewolves, there could be anything.

"He devoted his life to finding and killing them. He recruited others to help. They even had government funding."

I found that hard to believe. Then again . . .

"They became"—he gave a soft snort-laugh—"the special forces of monster hunters. The *Jager-Suchers.*"

"Translation?"

"Hunter-searchers, though Grandfather says the actual, correct German would be *Jager-Sucher,* no plural. Like deer in English, but the lack of a plural form for a plural force was confusing to the Americans."

My brain was clicking slower than usual, but it was still clicking.

Old guy. German. FaceTime.

"He's still alive."

"Edward's pretty hard to kill."

"Isn't he like, a hundred?"

"No one seems to know for sure, not even my grandmother."

"Also alive?"

"Yep."

"How?"

"My grandmother is a voodoo queen."

"Shut the fuck up!" I slapped my hand over my mouth. Hadn't meant for that to slip out.

"That's kind of what I said. Neither one of them goes into the field much anymore, obviously, but since they've stayed alive this long against ridiculous odds, I'm inclined to let them continue pulling the strings."

I would be too.

"I doubt they'll give up telling us what to do until they're in the ground." Ash's lips curved. "Maybe not even then."

Silence fell between us. This was a lot to take in.

"You're wondering if I'm crazy," Ash said.

"Wouldn't be the first time."

Now he laughed for real. Note to self: Laughter bouncing off stone prison cell walls sounds maniacal.

"We call the *Jager-Suchers* the family biz. In the past, Grandfather trained the new recruits, but now has anyone who plans to work in the biz join the Marines. The training is excellent."

Frankie had mentioned the Marines and Ash being a war hero. Apparently, that was true. Good to know.

"I served three tours in Afghanistan before I came home. Which is why, when there were whispers of a wolflike creature in the foothills dragging off children, killing old ones, changing young men and women into beings just like them, I got an express ticket right back to where I'd been."

"What was it?"

"*Qutrub*," he said in the same tone he might say *mosquito*. "Part demon, part jinn. Born of magic and a wolf."

"A genie?"

"A genie is a bright-blue Robin Williams, clever and quick, happy to grant three wishes. A jinn is a supernatural creature bound to its creator and responsible for misfortune, disease, possession. Likes to hang around graveyards and snack on corpses."

"Ew."

"Legends are often 'ew,' along with just plain terrifying."

As I wasn't certain what to say to that—what *could* I say?—I remained silent, and he moved on.

"My contact was Sahira. She had worked for Grandfather a long time. She took me to the village that had lost people most recently and showed me the wolf tracks that led into the foothills. There *are* wolves in Afghanistan, but"—he cleared his throat once, twice—"the ones leaving imprints that change from paws to feet are the ones I came to kill. So we waited all night and near dawn, when the sun paints everything glorious, the wolves slunk in."

"Then what?" I could see the wispy fingers of dawn floating over that foreign landscape and the shadows that slithered within.

"Then Sahira made the sign against the evil eye, and I

followed her as she followed them." He slammed a fist into his palm, rattling his chains, making me start. "She was a good fighter and—"

I noted the *was* and laid my hand on his arm, the movement causing a shot of pain through my wounded bicep. The bandage felt wet, but I was too big of a baby to check. What good would it do?

Ash took a shaky breath. "I hunted every night, kept at it all day."

"The day? When they're human?"

"They aren't ever human. Not once they've become a wolf."

"But—"

"Years back my aunt, maybe my step-aunt? Half-aunt? It's confusing, but she could cure them, however when she died, the cure died with her and now—" His blue-gray gaze pinned mine. "A werewolf is a werewolf is a werewolf. Forever. And silver works the same, regardless of their form."

In other words, he'd been waltzing around Afghanistan shooting people . . . wolves . . . wolf-people and watching them burn. I had to wonder how he'd avoided a concrete prison, a hangman's noose, or a padded cell this long.

Probably the abiding reach of *Grandfather.*

"The locals started calling me *qatal aldhiyb*, wolf killer."

Or maybe that was how. He'd become a hero. A legend.

"Things were going just fine until they weren't."

The problem with legends and heroes? They got noticed.

"You shot a person, and they went . . ." I made a motion with my hands to indicate *kaboom*. "Someone saw you, and they went ballistic."

"I'm better at my job than that."

"Then what could have gone wrong, oh great *qatal aldhiyb*?"

He shot me a disgusted glance, but I remained proud of my pronunciation.

"Then one of them got away."

"One?"

"It only takes one to spread the madness. Lycanthropy rolls out from the host like a virus."

"Damn lot of viruses going around," I muttered.

"You don't know the half of it."

And the not quite half that I knew, I would really like to unknow.

"We traced it to the States."

For an instant, I thought he meant the virus, and I guess he did since, to Ash, the werewolf was the virus and vice versa.

"I came back to finish what I started."

"How do you find a werewolf in a haystack?"

"That's what a special forces monster hunting family biz is for. I wasn't off the plane an hour when my sister told me she had a lead."

"Your sister hunts werewolves too?"

A shadow passed over his face. "Not anymore."

How could I have forgotten the question that had begun this conversation? His niece. Who must have been his sister's child.

"She asked me to come for dinner. Said we'd talk, make a plan."

He took a deep breath. This was going to be bad.

"The door stood open when I got there; the house was too still, and I could smell . . ." He grimaced. "My brother-in-law, my nephew were dead. They'd made it bloody." When he continued, his voice was faint; I leaned closer to hear the rest. "I had to shoot them to make sure they didn't rise and shift. I had to watch them burn."

"But they were dead."

"Those bitten by a *Qutrub* shift. Period. They aren't truly dead until they're shot with silver." The breath he released was as shaky as my own. "My sister was still conscious. Rose said that Haley hadn't been there for dinner; she was with friends. She'd walked in and seen the carnage, started to call Grandfather, then been hit in the back of the head by one of the guards that had remained human. Rose said the wolves had been sent by the *Qutrub* I'd let get away. She made me promise if—" His voice broke. "She begged me to—"

I thought of the rifle he'd pointed at the girl right after she'd said *Uncle Ash.* "She made you promise that you'd kill her daughter."

How could any mother do that? Then again, she believed the unbelievable; she'd watched the unwatchable; she knew her daughter would become a monster.

What would I do if that were me?

I didn't think I could ask my brother, if I'd had one, to kill my daughter after he'd had to kill what was left of my family and right before he would have to kill me.

Was that fair? Was that right? The rules . . . they were all fucked up.

I took Ash's hand, rattle, rattle went the chains, and when he looked at me, finally looked, he was *here*, he was no longer *there.* "Shouldn't you make certain Haley's one of them before"— instead of imitating the *kaboom* gesture—I was kinda over it—I waved my free hand—"you know."

"Grandfather would say 'better safe than sorry.'"

Grandfather sounded like a hoot.

"She didn't seem evil or soulless. She seemed brave and very sweet."

"If she'd seemed evil, if any of them had, would you have set them free?"

I frowned.

"In order to lull you, to get you to do what they want, they pretend to be human when they're anything but."

I remembered Haley's voice when she said *Uncle Ash*, brimming with love, hope, expectation. Was she that good of an actress? Was anyone? Knowing what her uncle was, would Haley walk toward him the way she had? Without my intervention, she'd have been dead or on fire. I would not feel guilty about saving her, saving all of them, until I watched them change, with my own eyes, from women to wolves, and do something unforgiveable.

"They took her for a reason," he continued. "Either to get me here and kill me . . ."

"Or?" I whispered, but I knew.

"Or to make me watch the little girl I loved turn into a monster, then change me too."

Ash seemed so tired and old, defeated. I tightened the fingers I'd at some point threaded through his. I couldn't help but lift my other hand and cup his cheek.

I offered my mouth, and this time he kissed me. Not too wet, not too hard or soft, but warm, so warm that some of the coldness I'd wrapped around myself to preserve every tendril of the past melted.

My fingers crept from his cheek to his neck so I could pull him closer, so I could just hold on. This kiss wasn't like the ones I remembered in my dreams, but it wasn't bad.

Or at least it wasn't until a sharp intake of breath, a startling *clatter-crash* was followed by—

"What the *hell*, Mom?"

SPIN THE FICKLE WHEEL OF FATE

I pushed against Ash's chest, would have scooted away if the collar around my neck hadn't hauled me right back.

Jenna stood in the doorway, at her feet an upended tray, sharp utensils, gauze, and tape spread across the concrete. A syringe rolled slowly in our direction, picking up speed as the poorly made floor canted downward.

She crouched, snatching at the first aid supplies before she glanced furtively over her shoulder, then whispered, "What are you doing here?"

"Looking for you."

Confusion washed over her face as she straightened. Several big, burly types appeared, and she stepped aside.

Something strange was going on, something I could not get my poor old mind around. Why was my daughter behaving as if she hadn't gone poof in the middle of the night, scared me half to death, then turned up in a werewolf hostel?

Two of the man-wolves hauled Ash to his feet while a third unlocked his chains. I was jealous until they dragged him away.

"Wait!" I shouted, but they did not. "Where are they taking him?"

"Who cares? He's a murderer, and you were kissing him!"

Since I had nothin' to explain why I'd been kissing Ash beyond fear, sympathy, fear, I went on the offensive. As a parent, I'd found it a good move.

"What was he supposed to do after they wiped out half his family?"

Uncertainty filtered over her face.

"They kidnapped Haley."

Something flickered in Jenna's eyes. Haley, she knew.

"His niece." Bet she hadn't known that. "They kidnapped those other girls, then they kidnapped you."

"They didn't kidnap me. I wanted to come."

"You . . . Wait. What?"

"Is that why you're here?" Jenna rolled her eyes the way she always had, and my teeth ground together the way they always had every time she'd done it. "You think I was kidnapped?"

"There's also the matter of the dirty, twitchy, terrified girl who showed up on my doorstep." Probably best not to mention how she'd come to be in my house, or what had happened to her after she'd left. "All she said was *no*, except when she was chanting your name."

Jenna! Jenna! Jenna!

"Any idea who she was?" I still wanted to let her family know she wasn't ever coming home.

Jenna shook her head. "I do my best to help them before they're—"

"Sold like cattle, like puppies, like"—my fingers fisted—"slaves."

"There's more to this than you know." She crouched again. "It's a long story, so let me check your wound while I tell it."

She tried to remove the makeshift bandage, but the blood had affixed the cloth to my skin tighter than superglue. She tugged, and I sucked breath through my teeth. That hurt almost as much as childbirth.

Jenna stepped into the hall, and water ran. She returned with a clean cloth and laid it over the bloody bandage. My head spun at the heat, the pain. I wanted to continue our conversation, except the sudden need to close my eyes and curse was undeniable.

Minutes, hours, eons later, she pulled what was left of my favorite shirt away from my skin. "Christ, Mom, that's a bullet hole."

"And your grandmother thought all the money we spent on your education would be wasted."

My mother. Not Patrick's. Mine had never let me forget how my behavior had embarrassed her, embarrassed my father.

"Didn't I tell you not to give away the milk for free?" had been her supportive response upon learning of my pregnancy.

Late nineties. Small town, Wisconsin. You do the math. My mom certainly had. Sure, I'd married a future senator, but I'd sort of had to. At the least her mortification had kept her from blabbing the truth; other people could do math too.

I'd hoped a grandchild—my parents' *only* grandchild—might have healed the rift. Not. Before Jenna could even walk, they'd sold out and moved to Tennessee. We'd barely heard from them since, and I was okay with that.

I wasn't sure why I was being pissy. I should be hugging my daughter, thrilled she wasn't buried in a hole somewhere. Or chewing on children. But since she'd seen me kissing Ash, she'd been a little pissy too.

"Did they tell you why they were sending you to the werewolf dungeon?" I asked.

"First aid on an intruder. No one told me that was my mother. Did they know?"

I shook my head.

Jenna frowned at the damage to my arm. "Who shot you?"

"It was an accident. I shoved Haley out the way and—"

"Her uncle shot you instead of her."

Guess that cat was out of the bag. I'm not sure I could have kept it in the bag since the truth wasn't difficult to figure out. Ash and I were the only "intruders," and he'd had the gun.

"Asshole," Jenna muttered.

"I stopped him."

"Doesn't make him any less of an asshole." Jenna jabbed the syringe into my skin way too near the hole.

I reared back, smacked my head against the concrete, and the chain on my dog-collar necklace jingled. "Did you just stab me with a knitting needle?"

"Don't be a baby. You want me to stitch that without a local?" She picked up the needle.

"No stitching. Nope. No. Uh-uh."

"You're bleeding too much not to have stitches."

"Great! Drive me to an ER." I tapped the lock on my restraint. "Got the key to this?"

"I do not. You gonna let me stitch you up and penicillin your ass, or are you gonna spin the fickle wheel of fate and see what type of infection kills you?"

Since she was able to talk, what came out of Jenna's mouth, more often than not, could easily have come from my own. But she was right about the chances of infection, especially in my lovely damp cell where the floor held grunge I couldn't identify, and the walls weren't much better.

"Fine. But I think you're grounded."

Jenna snorted and chose a suture.

"How can you be so calm?" I asked, voice hoarse and tight.

"What good does freaking out do?"

I wasn't sure, but I was really close to discovering the answer.

"This takes getting used to," she said, a lot less snotty than she'd spoken so far. "I know I'm being a bitch."

"Then stop."

Her lips tightened over what was, no doubt, another bitchy comment, then she let out a sharp huff. "These people are—"

"They aren't people."

"Mom—"

"Seems like you got used to werewolf world damn quick."

"I've been here before. I've known about the . . ." She searched for a word, then shrugged, and I was jealous. When you can't shrug, you suddenly realize how much you did and how much you liked to.

"Horrible, terrible, very bad, murderous, SOB werewolves?" I offered.

She cast me a sharp glance filled with exasperation. Nothing new there.

"There are two packs vying for territory, dominance, and—"

"Prizes?"

She ignored me. Probably for the best.

"One pack is different. More"—she rubbed her fingers together, searching again—"human, I guess."

Air blew through my lips, a derisive Bronx cheer. "And how did this pack of virtuous, *more-human* killing machines come to be?"

"Don't know, don't care. Just happy they did, otherwise I'd be one of them."

"What?" I ground my back teeth as my darling daughter stabbed her needle through my soul. Local anesthetic, my ass. "Why?"

"You think the pack that's evil would let us live once we knew what we know? We need the alpha of the"—she searched for a word and then just used mine, minus the sarcasm—"more-human pack to win or we're toast."

"And when you say toast, you mean dead? Changed? Sold into slavery?"

"Door number one, two, maybe all three."

"Then why bother to stitch me up, to 'penicillin my ass'?" I popped the *P* on penicillin.

"I do what I'm told."

Now I snorted, and she scowled.

"It never entered my head you might come looking for me."

"You left your goddamn phone at your apartment, then you didn't come back. What did you think was going to happen?"

"I—I—didn't think."

"Shocking."

She was being a pain, so I was being a pain right back. Call it motherhood.

"We can't bring our phones here. Nothing that might be tracked."

Silly me for not considering the werewolves might have forbidden cell phones at the werewolf rumble.

"I got caught up. This is so interesting, and I . . . just stayed. No one ever noticed before."

"Cammy said you always told her if you were going to be away."

"Cammy!" she said in the same tone Jerry Seinfeld always used for the name *Newman*.

"She was as worried about you as I was. Frankie too. The police not so much."

"Sheesh, Mom, did you put out an all-points bulletin, take an ad in the *New York Times*?" Jenna poked me again, and the world went red with dancing spots of black.

I decided not to mention her uncle's dipping into ViCAP.

"You disappeared from the security footage."

"What?" Her gaze on my wound, she didn't seem to be listening.

"At school. You left the veterinary sciences building and then poof."

"I didn't go poof. I came here."

"Then how—?"

"I don't know. They've got mad skills. You gotta keep still." Jenna's eyes narrowed; her teeth worried her top lip, an expression from childhood that made my eyes water, or maybe it was the instrument she kept jabbing through my flesh.

"You sure there was anything in that syringe?"

"Almost done."

"Promise?" I didn't hear her answer, if she even gave one, because those black dots slammed together, blotting out the red.

What felt like only an instant later, I heard a semi-frantic, "Mom?" Then, "Mom!"

Crack!

My check burned.

"Did you just slap me?" I opened my eyes as worry cleared from hers.

"Needed to be done."

I lifted the arm that wasn't on fire and placed my palm to my cheek. "That hurt."

She began to toss her implements of torture onto the tray. "Be happy I finished before I woke you."

"Whoopee." I let my hand fall back to my side.

"Listen, you wouldn't have passed out like that unless you'd lost a lot of blood, so you need to take it easy—"

"No problem there." I shook my head and rattled my chains. "How did you get involved with . . . whatever this is?"

She glanced over her shoulder, but whatever, whoever she was expecting hadn't materialized, so she answered.

"Dr. Maldonado, who will be my adviser next year, has been studying wolves as long as I've been fascinated with them."

In retrospect, we probably should have nipped that in the bud, though we had tried. Hence the therapy. But sometimes a parent is just glad their kid *has* an interest in anything that isn't sex, drugs, or rock 'n' roll. I'm sure my parents would have been thrilled if I'd been captured by any other interest but—

"The virus that's killed all the females was first found in gray wolves," Jenna continued. "The DNR had a fit. Without females, the gray wolf would have become extinct within a decade."

"So?"

"Haven't we been responsible for the willful extinguishment of enough animals? Besides, wolves help control mouse, rat, squirrel, rabbit, fox, coyote populations."

"Wouldn't other wolves, like . . ." I searched my mind for another breed of wolf. Despite Jenna's fascination, I knew little about them. "Timber wolves? Wouldn't they move into gray wolf territory and keep those populations manageable?"

"Timber wolves and gray wolves are the same species, so are tundra wolves and arctic wolves, which means the virus ran rampant, as viruses do, all over North America. Since 1985, when half the gray wolves in Wisconsin died from this disease, Dr. Maldonado has been studying it. That work has put Danny leagues ahead of every other veterinary virologist in the world."

I almost asked what a veterinary virologist was, but Jenna's use of *Danny* distracted me. I didn't like it. How far over the line that should exist between professor and student had they wandered?

"I wrote a paper about the treatment of viruses in animals, specifically wolves. My prof gave it to Dr. Maldonado. The DNR recently found a pack where the females tested positive for the 1985 virus in the boonies of the Northern Highland American Legion State Forest."

"After almost forty years? You gotta be kiddin' me."

"I wish I were. The DNR brought several females to the lab. As there wasn't much time between healthy wolf, sick wolf, and dead wolf, Danny asked me to help. When the subjects began to show signs of the virus, we injected them with the serum the doctor had been working on." My daughter smiled wider than I'd seen her smile in years. "They were all cured. Our experiment was a complete success."

"And what if it hadn't been? You, of all people, should have had the biggest hissy ever if wolves died."

"But they *didn't*," she said slowly for her idiot mother.

Kids never saw the danger in their actions; they only saw the results. Take my getting pregnant at eighteen, for instance.

"Still not understanding why you're *here*, Jenna."

"The virus jumped to werewolves."

"But they're not wolves."

"When they're wolves, they're wolves."

"Is a wolf that can't be killed with anything but silver really a wolf?" I asked, although they *were* dying by virus and apparently, somehow, by rumble too.

"We'll find out after the battle when I test the cure."

"Shouldn't your professor be the one to do that?"

Concern flickered in Jenna's eyes, followed by a pinch of her lips. "They . . . uh . . ." She wrung her hands. "They said one of us had to be collateral. I'm not sure what that means."

"I'm pretty sure it means if the serum doesn't work, they're gonna kill the mad scientist, then they're gonna kill you."

Probably me and Ash too, but I was getting used to the idea. I'd die for Jenna. But I didn't think the werewolves were going to let us make that trade—my life for hers. They didn't have to.

"Why on earth would your adviser agree to this?"

Had I asked that before? If I had, she hadn't answered.

"One of the alphas came to Dr. Maldonado and laid it all out. What they are, what was happening, then he asked for help to cure the females."

"Did he happen to mention how he'd *gotten* his females?"

"He did not." Jenna looked away for a moment, but not before the skin around her eyes tightened in a mini-wince. "He didn't mention a lot of things."

"And the doctor neglected to come to the conclusion that the guy who said he was a werewolf might be . . . oh, I don't know, insane?"

Impatience flashed in Jenna's eyes, tightening her voice. "You've seen them change, right?"

I nodded.

"Did *you* jump to the conclusion that *you* were crazy?"

"Yep," I said. "Batshit."

Jenna took a deep breath, let it out slowly, her face smoothing into the Zen expression I had always wanted for my own.

"What was Dr. Maldonado supposed to do?" she asked quietly. "Refuse to share a proven cure?"

"Not proven. Not yet."

"Within twenty-four hours of being bitten, they change. The virus attacks less than twenty-four hours after that, then they die. The injection will save them. I know it."

"Are you listening to yourself?"

Jenna flinched at the volume of my voice.

"You're ensuring that women changed into something vicious against their will stay that way. Against their will. Right before"— or was it after?—"they're sold into slavery."

"The other option is to die."

"Maybe they'd rather be dead. Did you ask them?"

Uncertainty replaced exasperation, and when Jenna spoke, it was so soft I barely heard her. "We cured the virus."

"You did, and saving wolves is something to be proud of. But these aren't wolves, Jenna."

"They are. When they're wolves, they're wolves," she repeated. "And that's why the cure will work."

"But when they're human, they're not human in the way they once were, are they?"

"I don't—"

"And if that's the case, then when they're wolves, they aren't exactly wolves and—"

The cell door clanged open. The same pumped-up dudes who had dragged away Ash marched inside, no doubt to drag me off, kill me, and toss me into the same ditch where they'd tossed him.

"Give me a kiss, sweetie. Quick like a bunny."

Jenna smiled at the words from her childhood. But she didn't kiss me—quick like a bunny or any other way. She stood in front of me and lifted her fists. I shouldn't have been touched. I shouldn't have been impressed. She was going to get her bell rung.

Or worse.

The faces of the man-wolves remained stoic. Could they laugh? Or cry? Experience *any* emotion?

Robot werewolves. A scary thought or a bad B movie. Patrick had *loved* bad B movies.

"It's okay, baby. Better me than you."

The robots didn't shove Jenna aside, beat her to the ground, or any of the actions I expected. Instead, each tucked a meaty hand under one of Jenna's arms and carted her toward the door.

I was so shocked I didn't scramble to my feet and try to follow until they were nearly through it. Then I shouted, "Hey!" and lunged after them, completely forgetting the steel dog collar around my neck, which jerked me into the air and tossed me to the concrete floor so hard Tweety Birds circled my head.

Never say I didn't give everything my best shot. Even being a senator's wife. I'd been a terrible one. But I *had* done the best I could.

"Don't worry." Jenna's voice became fainter and fainter as they towed my little girl farther and farther away. "They won't hurt me."

The door slammed behind them.

I stayed on the ground, trying to catch the breath that had been knocked out of me, not having much luck. Why would Jenna believe she was safe with these monsters? From what I'd seen, the only thing werewolves felt they owed humans was a horrible death or an equally horrible life.

Time passed. I felt woozy. Jenna *had* mentioned blood loss. Next thing I knew, the man-wolves were back, and the sun was either coming up or going down—hard to tell when I wasn't sure which direction the single window faced.

When they hauled me off too, I didn't struggle. Either they were taking me to my daughter, taking me to their leader, or taking me to my preordained meeting with a ditch.

I was able to cross off the last option—at least for the time being—when they deposited me in the same room as last night. A sense of déjà vu washed over me as my gaze went to the fight club arena.

Sharks? Check. Jets? Check. Prizes in cages? A few chained to the wall? Check and check.

They'd recaptured the girls. I hoped before they'd made a terrible mess.

My escorts tossed me into a corner, didn't even bother to chain me, which felt like an insult. No trouble with that one. Too old, too weak, too *hot once upon a time* to bother with.

A sudden commotion announced the arrival of Ash. They hadn't killed him, but considering his fat lip, steadily blackening eye, and shredded shirt stiff with blood, that wasn't for lack of trying.

Chains trailed from the wide steel bracelets encircling his wrists. Two goons used those chains to drag him across the floor. When he stumbled, they jerked him up by those chains too.

I thought about murder in a way I never had before. Torture. Blood. Lots of shiny, sharp silver.

Later. I needed to stay present. Escape was a remote chance, but if an opportunity presented itself, I should be ready.

As if my thoughts had conjured the opportunity, Ash head-butted the guard while he was fastening the chains to the wall. The guy stumbled back, and Ash sprinted for the door.

I did too. Why not?

Wait. Jenna.

The thought made me stutter-step, and the goons caught me.

The nose of the guard Ash had headbutted lay sideways; blood streamed over his lips, down his chin, tracing a river of red onto his blindingly white, one-size-too-small T-shirt. When the other arrived with Ash—he hadn't made it as far as the door, damn it—Broken Nose grabbed Ash by the throat.

"It's just your nose," his partner said. "Not like you were Olivier to begin with."

Olivier? What decade were they from?

"It'll heal the first time you change, so chill."

"I'll chill when he's dead." Broken Nose snarled like a wolf, though he still looked like a man. It was unsettling.

The two meatheads shackled Ash to the wall and walked away. Unshackled little me hurried to his side.

"They didn't chain you?" Ash massaged his throat where bright-red finger-shaped marks would become bruises. If he lived long enough.

"I guess I'm not much of a threat."

Although free like this, I could release Ash. My gaze flicked to the wall, but the hooks that once held keys were empty.

Ash shrugged. "Without my weapons, any attempt to escape isn't going to turn out any better than the last one just did."

"Why are we even breathing? I freed the prizes, you killed . . ." I threw out my hand in the direction of the rumble.

A smile ghosted his lips. "A few."

He had killed more than a few. Just as he'd killed more than a few before ever coming here.

"So why?"

"Badru, the white wolf, is a bit psychotic."

"And the other?"

"I don't know anything about him. He's the challenger. And no one's called him anything but Alpha."

Right. Mr. God Complex.

"Badru has been known to change hunters into wolves. Send us back where we came from and unleash very hard to kill weapons on the enemy."

"Sounds like Badru's a lot psychotic to me."

Ash lifted one shoulder, and his chains rattled. "Tomato, tom-ah-toe."

EVERYTHING'S SO
BAD IT'S HILARIOUS

"What the hell kind of name is Badru?"

"Arabic." Ash's hands fisted, released, fisted, released.

"Like *Qutrub*?"

He nodded. "Badru means 'born during the full moon.'"

State the obvious much?

"He's old, he's powerful, and so far he's been very hard to kill."

My hair stirred in an impossible breeze that smelled of sand and heat and ancient legends from a land far, far away.

I started as the loud rap music of yesterday, followed by a cheer, signaled the imminent resumption of the rumble. Fine by me. Sooner this crazy crap ended the better.

Although what would happen to us when it was through? What would happen to Jenna? Where *was* Jenna?

"Who's that?" I lifted my chin to indicate the same tall, fugly guy in the same custom-made suit who had been here yesterday.

"The Hakim. A wiseman."

"Wisemen don't shoot acid fog from their fingers like Spiderman shoots his web."

Ash's lips twitched. Almost coaxed a laugh that time. "The Hakim is also a sorcerer."

"Is Hakim his title or his name?"

"Sarah, please."

"Ash," I said quietly, and he looked at me, really looked at me, at last. "Talk to me."

I hadn't known him a week, but he heard what I didn't want to say. I was scared.

"I have no idea what his name is or if he ever had one in the first place. He's *the* Hakim. There is only one, and they are born into this world at the death of the other."

The crowd suddenly roared as the two wolves stalked into the ring. Wasn't a mark on them; all their scalded, torn, and missing parts were back where they'd been, which meant the broken nose Ash had given the guard earlier *was* a minor annoyance, easily healed. All he had to do was shape-shift. Big baby.

"What's our plan?"

Ash appeared to consider the question even as his gaze remained on the wolves. "I got nothin'."

"Nothing?" My voice wavered.

His breath whooshed. "They didn't chain you. You should get while the gettin's good."

My jaw tightened. "Not without my daughter."

He stared me down; I stared right back. He glanced away first, his gaze drawn again to the wolves as if they were lodestone. What difference did it make to a captured hunter and his accomplice who won? Sure, Jenna had said one of the packs was evil and the other not. But seriously? Werewolves. How not-evil could they be?

"If we hang on long enough, won't someone come looking for you?" The thought, hope, semi-prayer from someone who hadn't prayed in forever had been bubbling in my brain since Ash had told me about his family biz. "I mean, you told someone where you were going. Called for backup? Had a tracking chip implanted when you were born?"

"Yes, yes, and we aren't that crazy. Yet."

"So when's the cavalry coming?"

"I'm sure they came. I'm just as sure they saw nothing when they got here."

"How could they see nothing?" I threw my arm out to indicate all the *somethings* in the room.

"The Hakim is a sorcerer. He made sure the challenge would not be interrupted a second time."

"How'd we manage to interrupt it the first time?"

"Someone screwed up or we just got lucky."

"I don't feel very lucky."

"Neither do I."

Silence fell between us, but my thoughts wouldn't stop whirling. The females dying; Jenna being blamed, killed. Jenna becoming a werewolf. My becoming one too.

What would I look like with pointy ears, a snout, a tail?

A startled burst of laughter escaped. It was one of those "everything's so bad it's hilarious" laughs, an "if I don't laugh, I'll cry" laughs.

"What's so funny, dumbass?" Bottle Blondie asked.

I gave her the finger. Not in the mood.

She hit the door of her cage so hard I wouldn't have been surprised if it slammed open. I reared back, straight into Ash's lap. He grunted, and his chains jangled like the ghost of Marley's.

"Sarah," Ash murmured.

I turned in his arms, and my wound jingled with red-hot agony. But suddenly he wasn't watching the rumble; he was watching me, and the pain faded. I wrapped my fingers around his biceps and held on.

I'd been interested in Ash from the beginning. I'd blamed the yearning on my lack of sex for far too long. Who wouldn't? And that was part of it—the rest . . . I had to dig. He was good-looking. Hell. He was downright hot, head to toe. But he was also funny in a way I enjoyed, and he didn't kiss half-bad either.

I'd never thought I'd be attracted to a he-man who played with guns. However, when dealing with werewolves, alpha males —ha, ha—were probably the way to go. Bottom line, Ash knew the score, and it was comforting to someone who didn't. I was sorry we were probably going to die. I'd have enjoyed getting to know him. I'd have enjoyed . . .

Ash kissed me again. Yeah, this. *This*. Even lovelier than the last time, probably because it would be the last time.

My fingers, which had somehow crept slowly, carefully to his shoulders, tightened. Who'd have thought killing werewolves resulted in muscles like these? My thumbs caressed his collarbone, both smooth and so hard; he deepened the kiss.

"Jesus, get a room," another of the caged girls shouted. The rest of them laughed.

Ash pulled back.

"What's wrong?"

He slid me off his lap and onto the ground. "This isn't a good idea."

"I don't care if everyone's watching." There was something there, something between us I hadn't felt in years, decades, maybe ever. Not better, not worse, not weaker or stronger. Just . . . different.

"I don't care either." Ash touched my hair. It would have been heartbreakingly sweet and romantic if his manacles hadn't clocked me in the face.

"I'm sorry." His arm dropped. "We should probably—"

A growl rumbled low, furious, then one of the minions— where had he come from? They moved quieter than cats— snatched the chain latched to my collar and towed me after him. I fought—I did not want to be closer to the wolves, the battle, the Hakim—but it was like fighting a tide when you didn't know how to swim. Fruitless.

Half a dozen yards from the action, the guy kicked the back of my legs. My knees screamed when they collided with the stone. Ash landed at my side. I reached for his hand. His was even colder than my own, but his touch helped. I wasn't alone; neither was he.

The Hakim began his walk, encircling the participants in burning fog. He performed the same motion as before to begin the rumble, and the participants smashed into each other's chests, just like before. This time the black werewolf, Alpha, flew backward, landing on the concrete with a bone-crunching thud.

He got to his feet, shook his massive head, then staggered into the silvery mist.

Zzzt!

He spun away; his tail passed through, then started on fire.

Yoooooo-wl.

"That has to smart."

I heard the smile in Ash's voice.

Before Alpha even had a chance to stop, drop, roll, and put out his tail fire, Badru ducked in and made a grab for his throat. Alpha twisted and Badru yanked out a piece of his shoulder instead.

After that, I tried not to watch—claws slashed, blood flew, blood dripped, at one point blood spattered me in the face—but my eyes were drawn back to the bout like the proverbial train wreck. Chunks of fur smacked the ground, the thud solid enough to reveal those chunks were more than just fur.

The Sharks shouted; the Jets roared; the rap pounded. If either of the wolves made a sound—snarl, growl, whimper—no one would hear, no one would know. Did anyone care?

Though his tail had eventually stopped flaming, the brutal initial contact had caused the Alpha to move slower from the get-go, and Badru used his speed to take the advantage. He feinted, dodged, darted forward—nipping and tearing, tearing and nipping. Black fur glistened; the scent of blood mixed with the scent of burned tail. No one seemed to find that nauseating but me.

How long would this go on?

"If only silver or the virus kills werewolves, how does a fight to the death work?" I used the end of my no-longer-favorite shirt to scrub werewolf blood off my nose.

"They can't shift during combat, which means they can't heal. When one of them surrenders, the other ends it with silver."

I frowned. "What if neither of them surrenders?"

"Everyone surrenders. Eventually."

"Not me," I whispered, thinking of Jenna.

"Everyone. It's only a matter of time."

Badru became energized by the scent, the flow, the taste of blood. Sure, he had wounds—burnt-orange polka dots sprouted here and there upon the luminescent white fur—but they were nothing compared to those he had inflicted on the black wolf.

Only a matter of time.

As if I'd willed it, Alpha swayed, staggered. He had to be weak, dizzy with blood loss that could only be reversed by the magic of the change. When he stumbled, half the room gasped, and the other half cheered.

Badru took that cheer as encouragement and charged. Right before he would have hit Alpha and bowled him over, probably for good, Alpha tucked and rolled, the quickness of the movement a surprise considering his lethargy thus far. Even more surprising was the speed he used to snatch Badru's leg as he skidded by.

The crunch was drowned out by the cheers and the jeers and the music, but Badru's howl was loud enough to shatter the windows if there'd been any left in the place.

He landed on his side still snapping, snarling, fangs flashing bright. He got up, but his ruined leg pulled him back down, and this time he stayed there.

The rap music snapped off, and the silence that settled over the room pulsed.

"Is it over?" I whispered.

"Not yet."

The black wolf loomed over the white. Alpha lifted his paw, and moonlight sparked off razor-sharp claws. Badru snarled, snapped, and managed to open yet another wound in Alpha's chest, a tender area since he yipped.

Emboldened, Badru tried again to get up, but Alpha had had enough, same as me, and heaved a huge huff before slashing downward.

Belly opened, guts poured out. If I'd had anything to eat in the past few days, my guts would have been pouring out too. Small favors.

A cacophony of shouts ensued. One side begged for mercy, the other for victory with the same word.

Surrender!

Badru tilted his nose to the moon that ruled them, baring his throat to the conqueror.

The Hakim clapped, and the circle of fog poofed out, a final wisp of smoke curling around his wrist before disappearing on a nonexistent wind. He lifted a carved wooden box; inside a silver, bejeweled dagger rested on royal-purple velvet.

"How's he gonna use that without opposable thumbs?" I asked.

Alpha shook; droplets the shade of rubies pattered onto the cement. He twisted and turned as if he were stuck in a very tight space or perhaps bound in a very tight suit.

A werewolf suit.

I cough-laughed. At least no one heard me. They were too involved with the show.

Change seemed to happen between one blink and the next. What had been a paw was suddenly a hand. Where there had once been a tail, there was none. Quadruped became biped, one leg, one arm at a time, claws retracting to fingernails, toenails. Black fur shimmered too bright, forcing another blink, then hair of onyx threaded with sapphire rippled over shoulders that rippled too. The guy was built, at least from the rear view if you could ignore the wash of blood from his rapidly healing wounds.

The Hakim placed the knife in the victor's palm, then the alpha called Alpha took a knee and raised the weapon high.

Something about him caused a tingle to buzz at the tip of my spine.

"Almost over." Ash's hand tightened on mine.

Despite the hint, I still flinched when the blade swished downward, winced when it entered the throat dead center in one of the few still-white sections. It did not stay white for long.

As the wolf died, then shifted into a burly but buff man with short white hair, silver flares shot from his body and smacked into the chest of the kneeling man—*whap, whap, whap*—each flare causing him to jerk with its force. I waited for him to fall, but he did not.

"You said it was over."

"Almost," Ash repeated.

The flares kept coming, the man-wolf kept jerking as each slammed into his body and disappeared. Was I imagining that his muscles pulsed larger to the beat of a heart?

Eventually the light show slowed; a few sparks flew skyward like dying fireworks leaving behind nothing but a pile of dust and bone.

"What just happened?" I pressed closer to Ash, hoping his confidence, his competence, his courage might flow into me.

"Magic." Ash's whisper tickled my ear, stirred my hair.

Memory flickered. "A *Qutrub* is a jinn too."

"Part demon, part magic."

How could I have forgotten?

"To kill one is to take his magic, along with his life."

"If they're magic, then why clash like gladiators?" I asked.

"Like I said, they can't use their powers in a battle. Otherwise, they'd just regenerate forever, on and on, world without end."

"Who's gonna stop them?"

"The Hakim creates a charmed circle; he holds it free of any sorcery."

"What stops him from letting his alpha win?"

"The Hakim isn't a werewolf, so he has no alpha, no allegiance beyond the laws of pack. He is incorruptible."

In my experience, no one was incorruptible.

The Hakim swished his hand toward a hall that led deeper into the warehouse. "And now for the revelation."

Gooseflesh prickled at the sound of his voice—deep, smooth, mesmerizing, the accent just British enough to sound smart AF.

All eyes fixed on the utter darkness beyond the doorway. Nothing moved, or if it did, I sure couldn't see it. Everyone seemed to hold their breath, waiting for the revelation.

Instead, a man—old and stringy, bald too, face resembling a golden raisin left forever in the sun—slipped through.

"Wendell," Ash said, "the victor's second-in-command."

"Seriously?" How did that guy command anything?

"Looks are deceiving. Wendell was changed as an old man, but he has the strength, the viciousness, and the magic of a *Qutrub*."

Before I could ask anything else, one of the most beautiful creatures I'd ever seen emerged. Not that my life had been full of gorgeous men. The closest I'd ever gotten was a fundraiser attended by Brad Pitt. He had been *can't take your eyes off him* pretty, but this guy . . .

Imagine the face of Regé-Jean Page, skin and eyes a vista where desert meets the sky, framed by a waterfall of shining hair the shade of burnished copper, curly and tangled as Jason Momoa's, atop Deadpool's—I mean, Ryan Reynolds's—body and you get—

"Zane." Ash practically spat the word. "Badru's beta."

Ash hated him more than he'd hated any of the others, and it didn't take a rocket scientist to figure out why.

"He killed your family."

As it wasn't a question, Ash didn't answer.

"To the victor go the spoils." Zane's voice rose above the others, his accent only slightly less sexy than Antonio Banderas's. However, his wasn't Spanish. More like French, but not quite. "The prizes are yours. As are we."

He bowed so low his forehead nearly touched his knees. I could have done a world of yoga and never managed that.

Here, there among the crowd, the members of the losing pack did the same. When they straightened, their gazes returned to Zane, or maybe it wasn't him so much as whatever waited on the other end of the chain trailing from his long, supple fingers.

"And now for *pwi an,* the prize."

I thought there were *prizes.* Plural. Was it better or worse to be *the* prize?

"What language is that?" I asked.

"Haitian Creole, but sometimes he'll toss in some French just to sound more of a pretentious ass."

Zane swept his other hand in that direction too; the grace in the gesture reminded me of the hostesses on *The Price is Right.*

Janice, please show our contestants what they've won.

He yanked on that chain, and Jenna stumbled from the darkness, a collar around her neck.

"No," I whispered.

"Change her," Zane said. "Per the agreement, you must make the chosen one your luna. Tonight at the apex of this full moon."

"Wait!" My whisper had become a shout. I lurched to my feet. "Take me. Change *me!*"

"Sarah, don't!" Ash tried to grab my arm, then my chain, but he missed both as I left him behind.

I didn't care. All that mattered was Jenna. All that had ever mattered was her.

It wasn't until one of the Jets grabbed me around the waist and swung me away from Alpha, who still faced in the opposite direction, that I heard the laughter.

Zane's luscious lips curved. "The luna, she has many duties, but the most important is producing *ti bébé*, an heir."

"Fine. Great. All in," I said.

"But, Mom—" Jenna began, and I shot her the look I'd shot her the time she'd misbehaved at Christmas Eve mass.

Jenna went as silent now as she had then.

"Would you *préférer* this . . ." Zane brushed his ridiculously supple fingers over Jenna's dark hair. She flinched away, but he ignored her, bringing his fingertips to his nose. He shut his eyes and inhaled. His expression was ecstasy.

On the exhale, Zane's eyes—that eerie, wispy blue—opened and pinned me. I wanted to cringe, maybe cry; instead, I stood straighter and stared right back. I thought I saw a tinge of admiration, then it was gone too fast to be sure, and Zane's lip curled.

"Or would you *préférer*"—he flicked a finger at me—"that?"

I was old. I was dirty, bloody. I smelled. But I wasn't going to give up. Because I was a mother, and we just didn't.

"Take me," I repeated, and everyone laughed again.

The werewolf king lifted one arm, and silence descended. That silence thrummed, lengthened, threatened to go on forever and then—

"I accept."

The same tingle I'd had earlier raced up my spine, my neck, across my scalp. My hair hurt, almost as much as my chest. I took a step forward—mute, hypnotized.

"Mom?" Jenna said at the same time Ash said, "What is it?"

I didn't answer, couldn't, because my mouth had gone dry, my tongue too. I walked toward Alpha. No one stopped me.

Slowly, he turned. "Hello, Sunshine."

"Gideon," I whispered.

Then I fainted.

THE MOON CALLED

*G*ideon had been MIA since the night we'd painted our names on the rock at Lunar Lake.

There'd been other times he'd missed school. He couldn't stand by if anyone was being bullied, and as a result, he'd gotten into a few scrapes. There'd been detention and eventually a suspension. One jerk just wouldn't let up, and Gideon had knocked the asshole's block off. He might be slim and a little clumsy, but he knew how to punch. He'd been sick once or twice, even tripped and fallen down the stairs once. However, he'd always let me know where he was or what was wrong.

Nevertheless, I didn't worry until that one day had stretched into two; when it stretched to three, I called his house. No one had answered, and they weren't the sort of family to own an answering machine.

As the new guy in a town that rarely got them, Gideon hadn't made close friends. I approached the few boys he knew. Computer geeks. Chess club types. Outliers like him.

They hadn't seen Gideon either.

I went to his house, knocked, listened, knocked again, then I started pounding. I woke his father from what looked and smelled like a four-day bender.

"I don't keep tabs on 'im." He turned and shouted into the depths of the house. "You know where the kid is, Cherry?"

Mrs. Moran, whom I hadn't met any more than I'd met Mister despite my asking to, shouted, "No! Check with that princess from town he's fucking."

I winced. How did someone as sweet and gentle as Gideon come from people who were anything but?

"Is there some reason he'd want to disappear, girl?" Mr. Moran's beady gaze dropped to my stomach, and the rolling waves of nausea that had overtaken me the past few days rolled faster, harder.

I added one and one . . . came up with three, and when Gideon's father shut the door, I ran, didn't stop running, until I reached Patrick's house.

"I need a favor," I said as soon as he opened the door.

And that was how I ended up waiting in Patrick's car outside a pharmacy two towns north while he made the purchase, then peeing on a stick in my best friend's bathroom.

"Well?" Patrick asked when the required number of minutes had passed, plus five more.

I opened the door and showed him the stick with the two pink dots.

He knew what that meant since he'd read the instructions. My hands had been shaking too hard to see the words. "I suspected this."

How could he when I hadn't? Sure, I hadn't had a period in longer than a month, but I never did. A more erratic cycle than mine had never been seen by my doctor, unless it had been my mother's.

"And if I could, then so could he."

"You think Gideon left me?"

"Don't you?"

"No! He wouldn't. Not ever."

The last time I'd seen him, what he'd said, what I had.

Promise me nothing will ever keep us apart.

Nothing. Ever.

I'd believed him then; I believed him still.

"What are you going to do?" Patrick asked.

"I'm going to find Gideon."

But I couldn't. No one could.

Sure, they tried but not very hard. Especially since Gideon's parents believed he'd left on his own.

I begged the police chief to put out an APB, a call to the FBI. Something. Anything.

"Kids like him disappear," he said.

Except Gideon wasn't a kid. He was eighteen, and all evidence pointed to his walking away of his own free will.

"He'll turn up eventually."

Except he hadn't. Ever.

No one but me seemed to think that the complete disappearance of a sizable young man was strange. People did walk into the endless forest and never came back out. But why would he?

I might know in my heart that Gideon would never leave me, but I hadn't been able to prove it. Despite my age labeling me an adult in the eyes of the law, just like Gideon, I was a kid, having a kid, and I didn't have time to wait.

Thank God for Patrick. Without him, I'd have gone crazy. His family had lived in Lunar Lake so long no one really messed with them. Once Patrick's mom and my mother got together, they'd steamrolled me straight down the aisle. I was so thrilled to have someone care about me, want me, even need me, I'd allowed it to happen.

Patrick and I moved into his grandmother's house, and my in-laws proceeded to use their money and their influence to get Patrick elected first to the Wisconsin legislature, then to the federal. They also managed to smooth over any stories that might derail a political career in those backward, bygone days of yesteryear.

For instance, my husband was gay.

He was always discreet. So much so that I wasn't certain Jenna knew the truth.

My mother never forgave me, my father never forgot. I was going to be the first Jacobson to go to college, and I let a boy ruin it.

They'd warned me about Gideon from the moment I'd brought him home. He wasn't from Lunar Lake. He wasn't like the other boys who lived there. He'd break my heart.

True. True.

"True." I opened my eyes as the past gave way to a world gone mad. My daughter shouting, "Mom!" interspersed with, "Let me go, you son of a bitch!" that Ash punctuated every so often with, "Assholes!" and other endearments.

Chains rattled and clanked. The man-wolves growled, and the prizes howled, the sounds made stranger emanating from human throats.

"Quiet."

Gideon didn't shout, yet everyone went silent as if a great cloak of it had fallen over them. Considering the silver flares of magic I'd seen flying around, maybe one had.

I lay where I'd fallen. No one hovered nearby. The two who might have helped me were prevented from doing so by the minions holding their chains.

My daughter's eyes shone nearly black in her pale, pale face, while Ash's had narrowed to slits of ice and fury. His sweat-plastered silver-gold hair had gone the shade of rust-streaked chrome. Blood dripped from his manacles onto the floor.

Gideon rested a bare shoulder against a nearby wall as he observed the festivities. No one stood between us, and no one held on to *my* chains.

I rolled to a crouch, and my head swam. I'd probably knocked it on the concrete floor, at the least rattled my brains, at most given myself a brain bleed. Didn't matter. I'd sworn that if I ever saw him again—

I bolted, gritting my teeth against the dizziness, refusing to acknowledge any pain, in truth not feeling any because I had one thing, and one thing only, in mind.

Reaching Gideon.

I almost made it too. One more step and I'd have launched myself the rest of the way. Instead, someone caught my trailing chain, and my fingernails dug scarlet furrows from his thighs to his ankles.

Damn, I'd been aiming for his eyes.

"Bastard!" I shouted as I landed on my ass. "How could you? Why would you?"

Gideon tilted his head, staring at me as if I were an amusing bug on the end of a pin, one he'd very much like to pluck the wings from, one by one.

That look. It made me so mad. I leaped to my feet and gave trying to kill him another go.

Landed on my ass even harder that time, the impact starting up or maybe making worse the *thrum, thrum, thrum* in my head.

Above that *thrum*, I heard laughter once more. The werewolves still found me hilarious.

Sounds of amusement ceased when Gideon stopped lounging and straightened in a lithe, sinuous movement he never would have been able to perform back in the day. Then he'd still been learning to manage his big feet.

Now he moved like a wild animal—graceful, smooth—every limb in peaceful harmony, and those stringy teenage muscles had become those of a . . . whatever the hell he was. The size of those muscles, the addition of his grace were the only changes—besides being a werewolf—that I could see. Otherwise, he appeared the same as the day he'd walked out of my life.

When he'd been eighteen years old.

Gideon waited to speak until all eyes had turned to him, set by set, as if compelled to do whatever he wished. "Bring her to the lair."

"The what now?" I asked, but no one bothered to answer.

"This one was chosen!" Zane jerked Jenna's chain; she reeled backward and landed at his feet.

"Stop!" I bolted in her direction, only to get yanked again myself.

Gideon took a single step forward, and every werewolf

cringed, except Zane who defiantly met Gideon's blazing topaz gaze.

Hadn't his eyes once been plain old brown? His hair *had* been black, but I was pretty sure I'd have noticed sapphire highlights in the strands one of the multiple times I'd run my fingers through it.

Chalk up two more things that were different. I was sure I'd find others.

"She"—Zane yanked on Jenna's leash again, and I must have made some sound—a growl, a snarl—because he flicked a glance my way before he continued—"is the prize the Hakim chose."

Zane glanced at the Hakim for confirmation, maybe assistance, but the man merely watched, his face as expressive as a dead president on Mount Rushmore.

"Allowing the Hakim to choose, agreeing to abide by his choice was the *une entente*."

The werewolves shuffled and murmured, confused.

Zane rolled his eyes heavenward, then translated. "The agreement."

"Except you *gave* me the choice," Gideon said. "Would you prefer . . ." He pointed at Jenna. "Or . . .?" That finger slid to me.

Fury flashed across Zane's beautiful face. "That is not what I meant."

"Nevertheless, it's what you said."

"What I said"—Zane paused, seeming to have a hard time spitting the next words—"is irrelevant." The Jets began to whisper. Zane's glare silenced them. "The choice was the Hakim's, and he chose—"

His fingers tightened on Jenna's chain once more, but before he could yank it again, the Hakim spoke. "Alpha is right. You offered, he accepted. The deal is done."

Zane looked around for support, found none. Gideon's wolves nodded agreement; Badru's stared at their feet and said nothing, which said a lot.

"Bring her to the lair," Gideon repeated.

"*Non!*" Zane shouted.

"Jesus," Gideon muttered, and I nearly laughed. Zane really was a PITA.

I crossed my arms to stop their trembling, and Ash inched closer, set his hand on my shoulder.

The movement drew Gideon's eyes, and a growl rumbled around the room, though Gideon's lips remained as immobile as his throat, his face impassive. The sound, disembodied, carried the hum of a ventriloquist throwing his voice.

I stepped in front of Ash, lifted my arms, ignoring the way the movement made my wound whisper, and tried to make myself big. Could the barrier of my body stop Gideon from hurting him? I had no idea. Gideon was my first magic werewolf.

He was my first a lot of things.

I lifted my chin. "What are you going to do with him?"

"I know what I'd like to do," someone said.

I continued to hold Gideon's gaze, refusing to back down, refusing to say anything else until he did. There was power in silence, just as there was power in words.

Gideon lifted one eyebrow, which wasn't easy to do. I'd tried. "I'm not going to let him go."

"Damn right," another someone said.

"Are you going to change him and set him loose on your enemies?"

He tilted his head the way he always had when an idea intrigued him, and the Gideon I knew and the alpha I didn't merged, separated, merged. He wasn't Gideon, not really, not anymore, and I needed to remember that before I made a fool of myself all over again.

"It's not the worst idea in the world," Wendell said. "Two birds, one stone."

If Gideon's pack, and by extension, Gideon, was "good," shouldn't he think this idea *was* the worst in the world?

Gideon's beta waited for a decision. Everyone did. But Gideon seemed to be listening to something only he could hear. His gaze went distant, his expression anticipatory.

"Your Maj—" Wendell began.

Gideon swiped his hand as if swatting a fly, and his sycophant silenced; Gideon's endless eyes met mine. "It's time."

Hysteria threatened, but I would not let it fly free. Hysteria would not help. Nothing could.

"No, Sarah!" Ash struggled to be free, though what he thought he could do in a room full of man-wolves, I wasn't sure. "Once you change, I'll have to kill you."

Together, the Sharks and the Jets laughed.

"You aren't going to have a chance to kill anyone." The minion that held Ash's chain yanked it, then once he'd hit the ground, gave him a kick in the ribs for good measure.

"Hey!" I protested, but no one cared. Maybe once I was their luna, things would change. They'd better.

"Get him out of my sight." Gideon's voice cut through the jeers.

Would I ever see Ash again? It didn't look good.

I touched my fingertips to the lips Ash had kissed and offered them in his direction. Right before he disappeared from view, he smiled.

"Let's get this over with." I stepped toward the door.

"Lunas must be changed in the light of the full moon at midnight," Zane said. "In view of the entire pack."

"No thank you." Being changed—whatever that entailed—was bad enough. Being changed in front of these half-wild creatures . . . I could imagine nothing worse. Unless it was watching Jenna do it.

"So it is written in the *Book of Books*." The Hakim bowed his head. "So it will be done."

"The *Book of Books*?" I repeated. "You gotta be kiddin' me."

"Mom!" Jenna said urgently. "Shh!"

If my baby hadn't seemed so scared, I might have rolled my eyes. What good would shushing do us now? Probably as much good as talking had done so far.

"He's right." Gideon appeared as happy to admit that as he had agreeing to attend my mother's birthday brunch in an obviously secondhand, ill-fitting suit and out-of-date tie.

His gaze flicked to mine, and my cheeks went hot. Menopause or the effect of his continued nakedness, which he wore as easily as Frankie wore a hat?

I'd had sex with him—or the him he had been. Back then he'd been as timid about his body as I'd been about mine. Back then, his body hadn't been *this* body.

But neither was mine.

"Not in front of—" I choked on the next word, which had almost been *our*. "Not in front of my daughter." I lifted my eyes to Gideon's. "Please."

Gideon continued to stare at me with that bug-on-a-pin expression. Once I was like him, would I be able to tear it off? Would I still want to?

Time stretched; silence pulsed. Seconds, minutes, days later, he gave a barely perceptible nod, and several Sharks grabbed Jenna and dragged her away.

"Wait!" I shouted.

They did not wait.

"You have to let me say good-bye." Who knows what I'd be like tomorrow, if I'd even care about the child that had once been my everything.

"He does not have to do anything," Zane said.

I didn't even glance in his direction. I was so over that guy.

The minions carting Jenna away had nearly reached the arched doorway leading into one of the myriad halls that twisted and turned through this place like a maze. I took a step after her, then whirled on my handler before he could use my collar and leash to put me on my ass again. I wrapped my fingers around the chain. "Don't even think about it."

I jerked it as hard as I could, not really expecting him to release me but no longer caring either. I nearly fell all by myself when he let me go. As soon as I regained my balance, I followed that girl.

Jenna kicked and screamed, she twisted and turned, but her actions didn't cause the Sharks to lose a step.

A single snap of Gideon's fingers and they stopped so fast I plowed into one of them and landed on my backside. It was getting redundant.

Jenna threw herself into my arms. Her chains smacked my own with a dull *clack-clack*.

"Who is he to you?" Jenna's voice wobbled, and I suddenly understood the cliché *my blood ran cold* because ice crystals moved through my veins, causing an agony so frigid it burned. "You know him."

The last did not contain the lilt of a question but the weight of an accusation.

Should I lie or shouldn't I? This might be the last time I ever saw her, was most likely the last time I'd ever see her as the me I was now.

Would I care about her afterward? I couldn't fathom ever *not* caring, ever *not* loving her more than I'd ever loved anyone in my life.

Even him.

"I don't. Nope. Never saw that"—I flipped my hand dismissively at the *king*—"in my life."

My voice held the ring of truth. *This* Gideon I hadn't seen. *This* Gideon I did not know. Didn't *want* to know.

Jenna's suspicion flickered—there, gone, there . . . I'd never lied to her, that she knew about, and I wanted to keep it that way.

"Take her out in the forest," Zane ordered. "And—"

A current of air swirled. A hush fell. Gideon's eyes glowed topaz.

Zane began to choke. He clawed at his throat as his entire body levitated until he dangled several feet in the air.

"If I hear you give another order to *my* pack, ever," Gideon said in a voice so cold it made me shiver, "I'll consider it a challenge."

Zane's feet waved as if he had been shaken, then he tumbled to the concrete, gasping and massaging his neck. Fingerprints the shade of expensive burgundy flared on skin the shade of desert sand.

"Take her out and . . ."

A sob escaped before I could stop it, and Gideon shot me a disgusted glance before he finished. "Confine her safely in the laboratory."

"Why not send her home?"

Chill air stirred my hair, and I waited for invisible fingers to close around my throat. I should probably shut up, but I couldn't.

Gideon made an imperious *come* gesture to his wolves, and one of the few men not young and buff and spectacular separated from the crowd. His name was . . .

Come on, old lady brain! Something with a *W*.

Wendell!

He was what Ash had called the beta, the alpha's lieutenant, just as Zane had been Badru's beta. So what did that make Zane now?

SOL I hoped.

"Can Dr. Maldonado do the injections?"

My heart went *ba-ba-bump*. Maybe he *would* let Jenna go.

"The doctor is . . ." Wendell's head lowered. "No longer with us."

"Fuck-knuckle," I muttered.

"It doesn't matter, Mom." Jenna's hands tightened on my

arms. "Well, it does, but *listen*, you need to understand, the luna is the queen."

"Figured that." Though if Gideon thought I was joining him in the royal bed, he was mistaken.

"She is the mother of the pack."

"Got it."

Gideon Moran was also destined for disappointment if he thought I was going to produce an heir, and it would serve him right.

"She's the protector, a leader." Jenna huffed and got specific. "You get the injection first, Mom. You."

"Huh." Being the test dummy might go badly but— "Better me than you."

She made a frustrated, furious, exasperated sound. Wasn't the first time.

The minions began to move in.

"Kiss me, baby, quick like a bunny."

This time she did, and that pain in my chest . . . it was heartbreak. Apparently getting kidnapped, chained, threatened, and abused by werewolves was all we'd needed to heal our rift. Whatever it had been.

I wanted to ask, but now was not the time. Now there might never *be* a time. And maybe that was okay. Maybe that was how it should be. Maybe everyone needed to just let shit go.

We held hands until they pulled us apart, then she disappeared into the bowels of the building.

It occurred to me that I had no one's word but Gideon's that she would be safe, but I had nothing else, so I'd believe in it as long as I could.

Gideon stepped beneath the skylight, lifted his face, and the moon's cool, silvery-blue glow cascaded through the glass. He seemed to breathe the light; he shimmered with it.

"Come." His voice echoed with promise and power, trilling along my skin like his lips once had.

I wanted to take one of the fingers I'd kissed, then offered to Ash, and offer it to him in a different way, but I refrained. Though I did not want to come, I wanted to be made to do so even less.

Of my own free will, I stepped into the undulating moonlight. "Now what?"

I tried to speak with strength, to stand tall, to be brave, but my voice was a whisper, and I couldn't stop shaking.

"Shhh." The sound was a wind that whirled all around me.

Gideon flicked a finger as if he was flicking a bug, and the latch on my iron dog collar clicked open; my restraints fell away, clanging onto the ground near my feet. He waved a hand, and they whooshed away.

Nothing moved but that wind, which seemed to ruffle my hair, to taste of my lips the way he once had.

"Look at the moon, Sunshine, just . . . look at the moon, and everything will be all right."

The instant I did, I couldn't see anything *but* the moon. I didn't want to. The sheen was so bright my eyes watered, making Gideon no more than a shadow in the center of all that brilliance.

Sarah.

The moon called. She knew my name.

Gideon's breath, fiery hot, brushed the moon-chilled skin of my hand and drew my gaze from the silver-tinged sky to the great black wolf at my side. He nuzzled me for just an instant, and any fear I might have had melted away.

Until he bit me.

WHEN PREY RUNS, A
PREDATOR PURSUES

*T*he silvery glow tickled, then flared with both ice and heat.

"Why?" The sound of a voice, which was not my own but lower, guttural, and fierce, terrified me.

I knew why. Me for her, that had been the deal.

I managed to lift a hand, but it wasn't a hand, it was a paw because—

The moon . . . it—

"Ca-a-a-alls." Dear God, that had sounded like a howl.

Red-hot agony erupted outward, so strong I expected pieces of me to land everywhere. The shriek of something tearing made me skitter right before my spine bowed, contracted, bowed. I clamped my teeth. Wasn't easy. They felt too big, or maybe too many, for my mouth. Hands and feet became paws, arms became legs, nails became claws.

I sank those claws into the concrete, then I dragged them close. I was being torn apart, and tearing something else was . . . delicious. Twisting, I turned, shimmied, anything to make the burn if not go away, then at least burn hotter, burn faster, burn out. I hadn't felt pain like this since . . .

Almost there, Sarah, almost. Don't fight the pain and you'll meet your baby soon.

I tried. Really, I did. But when torment stabs you everywhere, when it *becomes* you, is it truly possible to give in? Doesn't everyone fight?

However, giving in then, accepting birth as the labor of love that it was, had worked. If only I'd listened at the beginning, I might have saved myself twenty hours of nasty-ass back pain.

I was willing to give anything a whirl, so I breathed in, breathed out—repeatedly—and after what seemed like decades—same as last time—something eased within me.

I was being reborn—of myself, of the pack, of him—into something more. I had to accept the change, embrace it as I'd once embraced my change from child to mother. Embrace this being born of pain as I'd once embraced another.

My muscles jumped beneath my skin, beneath my fur. As I became more aware of my body, I felt a horrible hunger, or maybe it was a terrible thirst.

Everything was brighter. Smells were smellier, sounds were . . . *wow* . . . a lot soundier.

I wanted. I needed. I had to have—

Meat. Blood. Preferably meaty blood. Bloody meat? I wasn't picky.

I took a sniff. Then a sniff, sniff, sniff. What I wanted and needed was nearby. I rolled onto my belly with a slow, rumbling *grrrr.*

"*Ya ibn el sharmouta!*" The speaker took a giant step—which really was a giant step with legs as long as his—backward.

The man-wolves formed a barrier between us. They were meat and blood and bone, but they were not what I craved.

I did my best to get my paws beneath me, but it wasn't easy with brand-new limbs—four instead of two—and that pulse of starvation not only in my head but also in my fangs and my claws and . . .

An itch started at the base of every hair on my body. I shook as if I'd just come out of the water, but that itch . . . it didn't go away. Neither did the hunger, which had deepened, the craving spreading outward until it seemed to blast hot and furious from the tip of my tail. I shrieked my fury to the heavens above, and somewhere nearby something, someone gasped.

A human, head and shoulders visible above those of the man-wolves before him. What was his name? Ah, yes . . .

Lunch.

"Time to go." The oldest of the man-wolves urged Lunch toward the hatch in the wall.

I began to slink forward. That line of man-wolves wasn't going to stop me. The only one that could stop me was—

The black wolf stepped in my way, and the old man shoved Lunch out the hatch, then slammed the door.

I howled, beyond angry, pushing the edges of sanity. Instinctively, I knew I wasn't supposed to kill the alpha, but that didn't mean I couldn't fuck him up a little.

A snarl tickled the base of my throat. He stepped closer; my ruff lifted; my fangs flashed. Then he touched his nose to mine, and the fury, the madness, the hunger simply . . . vanished.

Like magic.

The line of wolves parted; Gideon and I strolled through the door. The world outside was revealed like Oz had been to Dorothy, except in this world, our world, the darkness simmered; the sheen of the moon bubbled on top. The night embraced me, tickling at urges I couldn't quite name.

The moon bedazzled me. I came back to earth only when the rest of the pack—still human, but naked—joined us. They loped across the small stretch of grass between the rear of the warehouse and the forest, then leaped into the air as humans, coming down amid the shadows of the great trees as wolves.

The forest beckoned; the pack waited. The scent of evergreen welcomed us along with the flickering, cool, bright sheen of the moon. The urge to run was irresistible.

Gideon howled, the call so loud my ears rang. Wolves fanned out before us; as Alpha and Luna, we brought up the rear so that no danger could sneak up on our own. We would protect their flank, always.

How did I know this? Same as I'd known, even in the depths of madness, that I could not kill my alpha, my mate.

Instinct.

I followed the pack; I ran with the wind. It was enlightening, invigorating. It was everything.

How far did we go? Hard to say, but from the scent of the earth and the trees, we weren't in Kansas anymore.

I was a wolf, yet I could think like a human, remember Oz trivia and reason too. My brain was cooking with gas. Something I hadn't been able to say for a while now.

The pack slowed, paused, then parted to reveal . . .

Bleeeat!

A goat?

Grazing, not a care in the world.

The hunger that had vanished with Gideon's touch fluttered. Over two dozen huge heads swung in my direction. Gideon hip-checked me into the lead. Was this a test? Was I supposed to ignore the itch, resist the rumble?

I gave it a shot, but the goat caught a whiff of me as I wiggled and slithered and slunk in close, then lifted its head, took one look at me, and bolted.

Mistake.

When prey runs, a predator pursues. The chase was brief, the result inevitable.

The hunger that had sliced so deep became sated seconds after the kill. The others circled round, and I backed off.

Each wolf took only a single bite. Like communion.

Then we were running, the earth beneath our paws, the

wind in our fur, the moon lighting our way. We turned in a wide arc, and while a whine pushed at my throat—after being chained, confined, imprisoned, this freedom was delicious—I followed.

At the warehouse, we slipped inside, and the door closed behind us. My clothes lay in tatters, but they'd been headed for the rag bag anyway.

My fur, the same lovely shade of platinum I'd admired gracing the heads of fifties starlets in my mother's vintage movie magazines, gave off the scent of the forest as I shook away the dew that had caused several drops of dead-goat crimson on my paws to fade to carnation pink.

"Pay homage to your queen." Gideon waved a graceful hand in my direction, the smooth flow of his body a continual and startling contrast to my memories of the slightly gawky young man I had loved.

When had he shifted? How *did* one shift?

"Your Majesty." Wendell executed the same limber bow in my direction as Zane had earlier in Gideon's before he backed away. Hadn't seen him change either.

No one else had.

Gideon's ventriloquist's growl rumbled, growing, pulsing, becoming so loud I whined as the volume made my freshly minted werewolf ears throb.

Still, everyone remained exactly where they'd been, what they'd been.

"You heard Alpha!" For a wizened old man, Wendell could really put it out there.

Zane's appearance, fully clothed, had me mulling over the werewolves on our run. He hadn't been one of them, and when he spoke, I knew why. Zane was the fly in the ointment, the monkey in the wrench, the pain in my ass.

"Will you vow allegiance to the one who arrived with a hunter that mowed down dozens of our kind? You saw how she clung to him, how she held his hand, how they kissed. What will she do for him next?"

The wolves grumbled.

"I am her creator," Gideon said. "Her allegiance is no longer to him."

"It can't be if he is dead," Zane murmured.

Gideon shot him a scathing glance. Zane didn't seem to care.

I opened my mouth-snout, not exactly sure what I meant to do. Give a yip for attention? A bark for *behave yourself*? A snarl for *shut up*? What came out was a sharp whine that cascaded into a pathetic whimper and made everyone stare. And that was before I threw up the goat.

The nearest wolf backpedaled so fast he crashed into the one behind him. More wolves hit reverse, some snapped. Growls, snarls, yips commenced.

"Enough!" Gideon's voice was thunder. Everyone froze. Apparently, they were willing to do anything he ordered, except pledge allegiance to me. That would have to be dealt with, but not now.

"Get Jenna!"

"But—" Wendell began.

"Get. Jenna."

Wendell fled, and I staggered as a wave of dizziness hit me. Next thing I knew I was on the concrete, and I couldn't move, could barely breathe. Hot, then cold. Convulsions followed. I felt like my body was going to jerk and shake itself apart.

Jenna burst into the room. "Mom!"

I wanted to reach for her, but I didn't have hands. I still felt all the feels of love, of motherhood. In truth, I felt them more.

She pushed through the pack of wolves, and she wasn't nice about it. She was so strong. My little girl.

Jenna fell to her knees at my side, cursing beneath her breath as she fumbled with a syringe.

"Do it!" Gideon ordered.

Jenna glared; her expression was his. Had anyone else noticed?

"She shouldn't have the virus this soon!" Jenna's voice broke.

She was scared; I was too. If I died, would they then change her?

"She's the luna," Gideon said, as if that explained everything.

"Big, hairy deal."

"Yes. She is."

"You are *such* an asshole." Jenna pinched a fold of fur-covered skin and inserted the pointy end of the syringe.

Shining shit buckets! Didn't they have anything smaller around here than the knitting needle from hell?

The seizure passed. A sharp tingle crept through my blood, leaving behind a lethargy so strong that when I tried to move, I couldn't.

"Relax, Mom."

A snarl tickled my throat. How much more relaxed could I be?

"The cure works fast." Jenna bit her lip, a familiar tell that indicated she wasn't telling the whole truth. "You'll feel fine soon."

Considering I was the werewolf guinea pig, not to mention the first luna in . . . well, who knew, Jenna had no idea what the truth *was*, but I appreciated the effort she'd made to keep me from knowing I might die, even though I *did* know it.

My daughter began to stroke my head. I tried to remember the last time she'd voluntarily touched me. I didn't count how she'd thrown herself into my arms after the rumble. Was a terrorized hug technically a hug?

The tingling burn that had introduced the paralysis faded, not fast as Jenna had promised but . . . Had my ear twitched?

I tried to move my paw on command, got no more than a twitch there either.

"She's coming back."

And while Jenna's whisper sounded more like wishful thinking, perhaps a prayer if we'd been praying people, I held on to it with hope.

Another decade passed before I could make my leg obey my brain, but I did it. Another decade and I rolled onto my belly.

The wolves circled me, gazes avid. Were they waiting for me to die?

I came to my feet and stared them down.

Sorry to disappoint.

PACK WAS EVERYTHING

The blast-proof door opened and in strolled Triangle Head, behind him a line of females—the stolen young women in wolf form. From the speckles of blood dotting the dirty-dishwater fur of what I assumed to be Bottle Blondie, another of silver and gold who must be Haley, they had been on a similar journey to mine.

Moon. Shift. Bloodlust. Gideon's nose bump. Run. Goat. Or . . .

I sniffed the air. Nope, goat.

Time had passed while I'd been stricken. But the sight of them caused warmth to burst in my chest. I'd experienced the sensation once before, but when?

A girl stepped into the entrance to the room with the cages and that warmth expanded as did my memory. She was *my* girl—Jenna—and the first time I'd felt this way was the first time I'd held her in my arms. A combination of joy, pride, the need to protect her from any harm. A mother's love, and I felt it for each of them.

Concerned they would begin to convulse as I had, despite

Gideon's belief I had done so because of some magic luna dust, I took several steps toward them. However, Jenna was already there, syringe at the ready. One by one, she gave them the cure.

I held my breath, hoping, praying they would be all right. They were my children now. Pack was everything.

Gideon appeared at my side, again in wolf form. How much time had passed? Hard to say, though night still reined.

The pack parted like the proverbial Red Sea, spilling outward and leaving an aisle down which the females walked, single file in our direction.

I wasn't sure what I expected, but it wasn't the blinding flash of light erupting from their wolf suits, so bright I had to blink. Then, emerging from the milky dawn that trickled through the skylight, came Haley. No longer a wolf but a young girl.

Instead of bowing at the waist as Wendell had done, she took a knee before me and lowered her head. "You saved our lives by risking yours. I pledge my life to you." She lifted her head and lowered it once more in Gideon's direction. "And to you."

Gideon lifted his snout, the movement so minute it was barely a movement. Everyone looked to me, so I did the same.

Haley moved aside to allow the next girl to kneel, to pledge her life to us, and so on and so forth until the last girl came and went.

The parade paused.

My gaze slid to the males, and memory made my eyes narrow. They had refused to offer their allegiance earlier. That could not stand.

A growl rippled around the room, so vicious it seemed to take form and cause the fur along the backs of the wolves to ruffle. They dropped their gazes to the floor.

I didn't realize the growl had come from me until it stopped, and the lack of vibration in my throat tickled.

The males formed a line, walked through the dawn, shifted in an instant, then knelt and pledged their everything. They all addressed me the same.

Your Majesty.

None of them thought this odd, no one found their addressing me as *Your Majesty* as ridiculous as I did.

Sarah Sullivan, werewolf queen. I could rake in a million on the graphic novel.

The homage parade ended, and all eyes shifted to the rear as Gideon's snarl rippled in the air.

Zane emerged from the room with the cages—empty now— what had he been up to? Did he think we'd forget him if he stayed out of sight?

He was as gorgeous as a wolf as he'd been as a man, his fur a shimmering bronze, his eyes the shade of the sea. He prowled, slower than the slowest sloth, down the aisle in the center of the pack. *Zap!* He became a man, and I fought not to let my gaze linger on certain aspects of his physique. He was cut, ripped. Amazing.

Unlike me with my sagging . . . everything. Though not in this form where muscles rippled deliciously beneath silvery fur. Maybe I'd just stay like this forever.

"*Ou Majesté.*" Zane took the knee in front of me, bent his head so the reddish-brown fall of his hair sifted across his cheeks.

It bothered me that I couldn't see his eyes.

"I pledge my life to you."

I did the expected head bob. Then Zane lifted his head, and his expression . . . whatever it was . . . I didn't like it. He'd pledged his life. Same as all the others. And yet—

A skirmish broke out among the man-wolves.

"She's mine!"

"I saw her first."

"Fuck you."

"Fuck *you!*"

Blows commenced as Gideon strode into the light and came out the other side a human.

The sight of him naked made something in my chest tighten. While Gideon's body was different in many ways, it was the same in enough others to make me remember every inch of the body he'd had at eighteen. The first body I had loved. The body that had given me—

My gaze flicked to the last place I'd seen Jenna, but she was gone.

I bolted through the gray strand of dawn. The flash of light felt like the shock I received when I opened the milk refrigerator at the Piggly Wiggly—the zip of unexpected electricity followed by a short pulse of dull pain.

Except this pulse hit me like hail—*thunk, thunk thunk*—all over.

As if from a distant land, I heard Gideon snap, "You don't choose; *they* choose."

I staggered, and someone caught me.

"Mom! Are you okay?" Jenna tugged something soft around my shoulders.

I'd forgotten the naked part. I stuck my arms into the flannel shirt, which ended at mid-thigh, covering the still abundant—*damn it!*—curve of my ass, and buttoned it as fast as I could with shaking fingers.

I guess I hadn't eaten since—

Bleeeeeat!

I reached for Jenna, but she backed away. "Your hands."

Dried blood crusted my cuticles and stained my unpainted nails dead-goat pink. I put them behind my back.

"What did you do?"

I remembered the hunger that had overtaken me, the undeniable need to feed. On blood and meat. Bloody meat. "There was a goat, and I . . ."

"Oh my God, you didn't!" Jenna put her palms to her temples and pressed as if her head ached.

"I . . . did?" The declaration came out a question instead because I wasn't sure why she was so upset.

Her hands fell to her sides. I couldn't decipher her expression. Her fingers tightened, released, tightened again. "A goat without horns?"

I tried to remember what the animal had looked like. Brown and white, with a Billy goat gruff, though it hadn't been male. But horns?

I closed my eyes, pictured it again.

Bleeeat!

My eyes snapped open. "That's right. A goat without horns."

The blood drained from her face. I knew she loved animals, but—

"It was just a goat, Jenna."

"Just?" She bent at the waist and retched.

I leaped forward to do all the things I'd done when she was a child. Lay my hand on her forehead. Pull her hair away from her face.

"No!" She straightened. "D-d-don't touch me. Not with . . ." Jenna grimaced at my fingers. "Those."

I held them up in surrender.

She breathed in and out a few times. "I know you couldn't help it. That you became like this so I wouldn't have to, but . . . you killed someone."

"I did not! It *was* a goat."

"But . . ." Confusion flickered first in her eyes, then all over her face. "He said—"

"He who?" My tone had gone as chilly as a December dawn in Lunar Lake. Ice bobbed beneath the surface as well, sharp as knives, deadly to the unwary.

Jenna's eyes went wide, and any color she'd recovered faded.

"*Sa ta dwe mwen.*" Zane's breath brushed my ear. "That would be me."

The hair on the back of my neck ruffled. If I'd been a wolf, I would have snarled. Where had he come from? I wanted to whirl, step back, put distance between us, but that would show vulnerability, and I knew better.

Instead, I continued to speak in my newly discovered ice-beneath-the-surface voice. "You told my daughter I killed someone?"

"*Mais non!*" He slid around me; I slid between him and Jenna. "I translated the term *cabrit sans cor'*, goat without horns, which originated in Haiti where I was born." He sighed. "So very long ago."

My eyebrows drew together. "How long?"

Unlike Gideon, who still appeared eighteen, Zane appeared to be in his midthirties—the small crinkles around the eyes, the few lines framing his mouth did not detract from his annoyingly beautiful face.

"Once you are past the first century, they all blend together."

I couldn't tell if he was serious, decided I didn't care. "Why would a term like that even come up?"

"We were discussing the past. The way things . . ." His smile deepened. "Change. Forgive the confusion."

I didn't think it had been a confusion. I think he'd done it on purpose to cause problems and see where they led.

"Mom?"

Had I been growling? From her wary tone, maybe.

Zane inched to the left as if to give us privacy, but since he hadn't moved *that* far, I didn't buy it. I pivoted so I could see Jenna and keep an eye on him. Wasn't turning my back on that guy.

At my sudden movement, Jenna took two quick steps away, and I nearly reached for her before I remembered how badly I needed a shower and a nail brush. Instead, I clenched my hands and stayed where I was.

"I did not kill a person. I killed a goat. And from now on, when he tells you something, don't listen."

Zane's lips curved. Little fucker.

"Okay." Jenna's gaze flicked between Zane and me. "I have to go."

"Home?"

It was what I'd hoped for, begged for, nearly died for, but the thought of her leaving, of there being a bigger cavern between us now than there'd been yesterday, made my eyes moist. I would have swiped my tears away if I wasn't afraid I'd leave pink streaks across my face. I didn't want *that* to be her last sight of me.

"Not home," she said. "Not yet. They found others." She indicated the now empty cages. "Badru and his boys were busy."

"Asshole."

"Evil werewolf, so yeah."

Silence settled between us.

"I should," Jenna began at the same time I said, "We need to talk about—"

"A lot," she interrupted.

"So much." What had gone wrong with us? When? Why? Where would we go from here? How would I get her the hell out for good?

"I'll be back." Jenna hesitated, her movements jerky—go, stop, go, hesitate. She settled for a quick tap on the arm with the bullet hole.

Except the bullet hole was gone.

I nearly asked Jenna if she'd like to pat me on the head and say, "good dog," but I held that pithy comment within. Instead, an overprotective-mother comment slipped out. "Maybe I should go with you."

Jenna rolled her eyes the way she'd rolled them at me for years, and it gave me hope we could get back to the way we had been. Right now, her annoyance with me was better than a fear of me.

"I'll be fine, Mom." She hurried to join Dirty Blond and Freckles—I should probably learn their names—who waited at the door.

"Yes, she will be fine, *Manman*."

Was Zane going to start calling me *Mom* now? Would everyone? I'd thought *Your Majesty* was ridiculous, but I preferred it to that.

"You are the luna; she is your child. No one would dare to harm her."

"You'd better be right."

"I am."

I waited for him to take his leave or whatever they called it. My experience with titles like *Your Majesty* was confined to a binge-watch of *Bridgerton*. I needed a tutor in the art of werewolf royalty.

"And the phrase *goat without horns*? How did you know it?"

"As I said, the term's origin is in the land where I was born, and I learned it at my *grand-mère*'s knee. Who knew it, of course, because she was a mambo."

"Of course," I echoed, then my brain caught up to my ears. "A what?"

"A priestess, in the English, a sorceress."

"Huh."

"Huh, indeed." His smile deepened. "How do you think I became the way I am?"

"You were bitten by a *Qutrub*."

He laughed, and I felt Gideon glance our way. His growl didn't trill across the room. Yet. But it was coming.

"How odd would it be if a jinn from . . ."

He moved his artist's hands in a way that captivated the gaze. Were they all this damn graceful? Would I be?

"From across the sand and the sea, sired every werewolf

across every land. *Mais non!* Each culture possesses a shifter legend."

"So not all werewolves are magic?"

"To change from human to wolf is magic in and of itself, no?"

I wasn't sure if I was supposed to answer *yay* or *nay* to that, so I said nothing.

"However, you are correct. The type of magic possessed by those in this place *is* special. My *grand-mère* combined her power with a werewolf and *voilà*." He flicked his slim fingers outward. "Loup-garou."

Zane was a loup-garou not a *Qutrub*. I filed that tidbit away for later.

"Why are those in this place so special?"

"Because of the great magic used at our inception"—he indicated the pack, which had stopped fighting long enough to find their clothes and step into them—"we can procreate."

"Wait . . . What? Other werewolves can't?"

"Most strains are unable to even touch each other without"— he touched his forehead and winced—"*yon maltèt*."

"Headache?"

"*Oui*." Zane tossed his head, and his thick, full mane swirled like the model in a vintage shampoo commercial.

Don't hate me because I'm beautiful.

No problem. Plenty of other reasons to hate him.

"No wonder Ash really, really loathes you guys."

Zane's eyes shifted from ocean beneath the sun to storm-tossed waves. "The feeling *est mutuel*."

"How many strains of werewolf can make—"

"*Ti bébé?*" He tilted his head. "Beings like the loup-garou, like me, are rare."

"The *Qutrub* doesn't seem rare."

"Badru made many, many wolves."

"And Gideon?"

"Ah, yes. You whispered his true name right before . . ." His smile gave me a chill. "We do not know him by *Gideon*."

"Fine. Alpha. *His Majesty*." I twisted the final two words so they were more sarcastic than deferential.

Zane appeared to enjoy my disrespect, which meant I needed to tuck that beneath with everything else.

"His *père*, his father, his sire, Emir, made many wolves too."

I went silent digesting that. It wasn't long before another question popped up, and since Zane was being chatty, I asked it. I'd find out how much of this was truth and what was a lie later.

"If werewolves can be made by biting, why bother with"—I stifled my grimace—"cubs?"

Zane shook his head. "Cubs is so last century. The term is pups."

Still, ew.

"There is strength in numbers. And mates, pups, *manmans*, *papas*, *grandparan*, they make *yon fanmi*. Those bonds are even stronger than the bonds of pack."

"What's your magic?"

"*Ou Majesté*." He bowed his head, but when he lifted it, his eyes had become again an ocean of storm-tossed blue. "I know you are new to this world, but that question is considered rude."

"Whoops," I said, but I held his gaze, and I refused to step back, though I wanted to.

"I told you, I can procreate." His lips tilted, and his eyes swept over me in a way a man's eyes had not for a long time.

I knew what he was doing, and yet . . . I shivered as if his gorgeous hands had touched me and not his ridiculously beautiful eyes. The real issue? I liked it. And because of that, I moved on.

"What happened to Gideon's sire?"

"What usually happens to alphas." Zane's gaze returned to his new alpha. "They are challenged, either from within or without, and they lose. The one you know as Gideon was the beta for his *bondye papa.* No one knew Emir held the power to make wolves less vicious."

I remembered the insanity that had overtaken me. *Meat. Blood. Bloody meat*—and then I remembered the sanity brought by the nose bump.

"Why would no one know that?"

"Emir also absorbed that power in the ring. He didn't want it; he didn't use it. Ever."

"Ever?" My voice shook.

Zane shook his head. His gaze was solemn, but beneath I knew he was laughing. Because if Gideon's sire had never given him an anti-vicious-evil-bastard nose bump, then Gideon had been a vicious, evil bastard too. At least until he killed the man. The wolf.

The man-wolf.

"Emir's pack, *Gideon's* pack now, holds the territory to the north. Alpha waited for a time after he defeated Emir, then came here; he challenged Badru, and you know the rest."

My head spun, but I needed to learn, and retain, as much as possible before Gideon called a halt to this chat. Which, from his blazing glances in our direction, would be soon.

"If they're all *Qutrub*, what are you doing with them?"

"Sigma wolves . . . lone wolves are often killed if they encounter an alpha, but if they have a use, sigmas can be taken in. I may be different from the *Qutrub*, but I am also like them enough to have a place. I was strong enough to become a beta, which Badru was in desperate need of at the time. There'd been a hunter." Zane tossed supple fingers up and away. "*Sa se lavi.* Most sigmas don't end up second-in-command, but most are not me."

He wasn't going to care for being out of a job.

"How does one become a beta?"

"Promotion." Zane's eyes flicked to the pack as Wendell held up both hands for silence.

The old man had to have crawled on top a milk carton or two

so everyone could see him. Wendell was efficient, and despite his appearance, his apparent weakness, I didn't see Gideon promoting Zane over Wendell. Ever.

"If that fails . . ." Zane did a Gallic shrug, then walked off. Instead of joining the others, he hovered on the outskirts. As lone wolves do.

I'd looked up the definition of Gallic shrug once. The translation had been *shit happens*.

In this case . . . I wondered if *shit* meant *murder*.

A KISS FOR THE DYING

"*Y*our Majesty?" Haley hovered near, head lowered.

"You don't have to call me that."

"You're my luna, my queen."

"Which means I can say 'don't call me that,' and you don't call me that, right?"

Haley's head came up, and her gray-blue eyes flicked to mine. I smiled, pleased when she didn't look away. "Yes, Your Maj—I mean, Mrs. Sullivan."

"Sarah. Please. I insist."

"That's too familiar, Your—"

"Fine. Call me Luna." I'd never much liked the name Sarah anyway. "Okay?"

She nodded.

"Tell the others." I lowered my voice to a stage whisper. "Spread the word."

Haley's lips curved, and I saw the girl she'd once been. Could she be that girl again despite this?

"Is there anything I can do for you?" I asked. "Anything you want, need that I can make happen?"

"Alpha wants me to take you back to his quarters."

I snorted. "I bet he does."

Haley's eyes widened, and she glanced at Alpha who, for once, was not paying me any mind. He was still occupied smoothing over the chest-bumping, male-posturing pack members' argument over the women.

"He said you'd want a shower, some new clothes."

I was both annoyed with Gideon for telling her what I wanted and annoyed with myself for wanting it.

"Great." I tugged the flannel shirt closer. "After you."

She sprang for the doorway, and her silvery-gold hair flowed backward like a flag; a tickle started up in my brain. The instant we were far enough down the corridor where I could no longer hear the pack, and I hoped they could not hear me, I caught up to Haley. "Your uncle."

Haley's eyes welled. Damn. They'd already killed him.

"He's in his cell."

"He's okay?"

Haley swiped at her eyes. "He's alive. For now. They let me see him before I . . ." She motioned toward herself.

They'd let her see him before she changed. More mental torture for the hunter or an act of kindness? Former. Definitely.

"He's to be executed in front of the entire pack."

I very nearly asked how, but I didn't need that nightmare in my head. Yet. I'm sure it would be there forever once I saw it in bright, bloody color.

"He w—" I'd been close to saying *he wouldn't*, that *Gideon* wouldn't, but he wasn't really Gideon, was he? I placed a hand on her arm, and we paused. "I'll talk to him."

"It won't matter."

I'd still try.

"How is your uncle otherwise?"

"He . . . he . . ." She hunched.

"Tell me."

"He isn't great. He can't—" Her voice broke, and she took

a second during which I imagined terrible things, something I'd always been good at. "He can't heal like they . . . like *we* can."

"Take me to him."

"But—"

"Now." I used my ice-beneath-the-surface voice, and Haley straightened, bowed her head, and said, "Yes, Your—"

I cleared my throat.

"Luna."

She took off at a brisk pace. Right turn. Left turn. Left turn. How big was this building? Then another right turn, and suddenly there it was. The dungeon.

Cobalt-colored clouds clustered in the sky allowing only a gray, watery daylight through the single window. Ash's back was propped against the wall; he'd slid sideways, unconscious. The only thing keeping him from falling to the ground was the chain attached to the wall, attached to the dog collar that encircled his neck, beneath which I could see the finger-shaped bruises I'd predicted, as well as the scrapes and scratches that had come from his attempts at escape.

I wrapped my fingers around the bars and rattled his cage. Ash didn't move.

"The key?"

Haley's finger appeared in front of my face, indicating the key on the hook, on the wall, just out of reach.

Sheesh, they were assholes!

"Maybe you should . . ." I made a *run along* gesture with my hands.

Haley shook her head. "I'm supposed to—"

"Take me to your leader." Or at least her leader's lair. "I know. Go somewhere else and come back in ten minutes."

Still she hesitated.

"Haley—" I began, and she hung her head, but she left.

Seeing Ash like this . . . it made me feel helpless. Hopeless.

Weak. And the new wolf inside me sniffed around the edges of that weakness and smiled.

Whoa! Where had that come from? I wasn't sure, but I felt her there, waiting. Would the wolf chip away at what was left of me, take over, become me—always—if I wasn't strong enough to stop it?

I snatched the key, opened the door, and went inside. Kneeling, I pushed his hair, matted with dirt and blood, away from his face to reveal a lot more dirt, a lot more blood—dried and crusty and flaking like the blood on my hands. I resisted the urge to stick them behind me. I doubted he'd be able to see much with both eyes so swollen, the skin around them resembling rotting grape pulp.

I took his hand, and before he even hissed in a breath, I felt its wrongness, the brokenness inside.

"It'll be okay," I said. To him or to myself? Either way, it wouldn't be okay, and we both knew it.

His sardonic laugh was cut short as he flinched. "Man, that hurts." He sat up, arm sheltering his middle.

"Why didn't they send Jenna?" It occurred to me that *I* could send Jenna once she returned.

"They aren't going to waste her time on a dead man."

"Oh, Ash." I had to get him out of here.

He peeked at me through one eye. "How do you know him?"

"Huh? Who?"

Ash just waited and my mind scrambled. Should I tell the truth about Gideon? Probably not.

On the heels of that thought came footsteps.

"Minions," Ash muttered. "Goody."

Two Cro-Magnon types appeared in the hall. Had Haley tattled to Gideon, to Wendell? Hard to say, but as they didn't attempt to drag me out by my hair, I stayed where I was.

Ash let his eyes close. Had to hurt like hell to keep them open all swollen like that. They looked . . . heavy.

"I failed," he said.

"To save Haley?"

Ash gave a twitch of the shoulder, his nonanswer reminding me he hadn't come to *save* Haley but—

"To kill her."

"It's the same thing."

"No, Ash, it isn't."

"I'm not going to be able to do either one, so when I meet her mother, *if* I meet her mother, once I'm dead, I'll have to admit I broke my promise. Then again, maybe breaking my promise will mean I won't meet her, and I won't have to confess. I doubt men like me get to go to the same place as women like her."

"You're being morbid."

"What better time?"

I touched the back of my hand to his forehead, but I couldn't tell if he was feverish. A better thermometer had always been my lips, so I leaned in.

Both eyes opened, just a little, and Ash tilted back his head. "A kiss for the dying?"

"Shh." I leaned closer, and my breasts brushed his chest. The idea of touching my lips to his forehead as if he were a child disappeared.

His eyes slid closed. I pressed my mouth to his, lightly, I didn't want to hurt him. I wanted to heal him, to help him, though I knew I couldn't do either. The kiss was meant as a balm, but he tasted so good. He tasted like blood, and my wolf, well . . . she got interested.

My palms rested on his chest; my fingertips inched beneath what was left of his shirt and traced his collarbone, even as my tongue traced his lips. The wolf rumbled, dangerously close to the surface. I had to stop before she broke free.

I pulled back. "You're not dying."

He gave me a pirate squint. "Is that a statement, a lie, or a promise?"

I opened my mouth to say . . . what? . . . but I never got the chance.

"Lie," Gideon said. "Definitely."

I stiffened, straightened, turned.

At least he'd put on pants, hadn't bothered with a shirt. He lounged in the doorway all muscles and newfound grace, the cold, arrogant, *fuck you* expression I already loathed firmly in place. Gideon Moran had been warm, sweet, a bit shy, a tad gawky, but a *fuck you* expression? He wouldn't have known how.

"Let's go, Sarah."

I gave him the finger. When he laughed, I gave him two.

"You want me to have you dragged out?"

The minions, hovering behind, perked up.

I set my fisted hands on my hips. "Why don't you be a big boy and do it yourself?"

He surprised me by actually doing it, and he moved a lot faster than he had as a boy—he was a lot more everything than he'd been as a boy—I didn't have a second to prepare a plan. What would it have been?

He lifted me off my feet and bodily relocated me in the hall, then he slammed the door behind us. With his mind.

"I didn't kill your mate," Ash said softly.

The entire world stilled.

Heat pulsed outward as fury washed across Gideon's face. I stepped between him and the cell.

"Bring her." Gideon's exhale held a hint of dragon fire, then he stalked away without a backward glance.

He might bear a resemblance to the boy he had once been, but he wasn't. He had become Alpha, a magical, powerful leader of supernatural wolves.

And he was dangerous.

I held up one hand in a "stay" gesture at the minions who still stood on either side of the cell door. They didn't move back, but they didn't move forward either.

"Do anything you can to avoid being changed, Sarah. Once you're like them, it's over."

I froze, my mouth opening and shutting with no words coming out. Luckily, I still faced away from Ash and toward the minions. Luckily, they continued to behave like robots and did not react to his revelation.

He still believed me to be uncompromised, unchanged, unbitten. If I'd have thought with more than my body, if I hadn't been distracted by my wolf, I'd have realized before now that he never would have kissed me if he knew the truth. Should I tell him that ship had sailed, or shouldn't I?

Shouldn't.

If he got out of there—wasn't happening, but still *if*—Ash would come after me because a werewolf was a werewolf was a werewolf, right? I'd keep that truth to myself. If he died, let him die thinking maybe I had not been changed. What could it hurt?

I hated that my last memory of him would be the bloody, broken man I had abandoned. But I couldn't face him; I couldn't speak, afraid my voice would break on both the lie and good-bye.

The minions each reached for an arm. I lifted my lip, a snarl without sound, and they dropped their hands as if I were a hot potato. One fell in behind me, the other led the way.

Did they think I would run? Where would I go? Back to my lonely senator's widow life?

I could. Jenna would be the only person who might notice my absence on certain nights, and then only because she knew to look. I doubted Frankie or Joe—

Shit. Frankie. Joe. They were probably searching for both Jenna *and* me even now. What would we tell them if we suddenly reappeared as if nothing had happened? Alien abduction?

My escorts paused at an open doorway. Gideon stood in the center of his room. I stepped inside and closed the door in the closest minion's face. God, it felt good.

Still and quiet, Gideon waited. I wasn't sure what to say, what to ask, what to do first. Then words just popped out. "You had a mate?"

Gideon lifted his eyebrows. "You had a husband."

"Did you love her?"

"Did you love Patrick?"

"Of course, but not—" I stopped myself before I said too much. The nature of my marriage was something I did not discuss, *would not* discuss. Patrick might be gone, but his secret would always be safe with me. He had made certain that both Jenna and I would be safe with him.

Gideon stepped closer, and I fought the urge to inch away as heat pulsed off him like a furnace. "But not what, Sarah? The way I loved her? The way I would have loved my heir if my mate had been allowed to give birth to him or to her before the hunter killed them both?"

I flinched. "She was—"

"Pregnant. And I didn't protect her."

"What was her name?"

He glanced at me through the curtain of his overly long hair. "Katherine."

I wanted to ask so many things. How had he met her? How long were they mates? Was she beautiful? Did she love him even half as much as I had?

Instead, I just said, "I'm sorry." I should have stopped there. "It wasn't Ash."

Fire blazed at the center of his eyes. "You believe that because he said so? Lying would mean nothing to a murderer."

"He believes he's killing beings that no longer have a soul."

"Do you feel as if your soul has shriveled up and died between yesterday and today?"

"I didn't exactly feel my soul to begin with." Does anyone? "What I feel . . . what I *felt* after the pain was hungry and vicious with it." At least until he'd nose-bumped me.

"Changing from human to wolf only hurts the first time."

"Because I was reborn."

It wasn't a question, but he answered me anyway. "As a wolf. Yes."

"And that hunger?" The pulse I had felt in my brain and my blood had been irresistible.

"My magic takes that away."

"Nose bump," I murmured, and he nodded. "Every full moon you have to nose-bump everyone?"

"Just once."

"Quite a handy magic power."

"If the one who possesses it is willing to use it."

I remembered what Zane had said about Emir. No wonder Ash didn't believe Gideon's assertion that he and his pack were the good guys. I wasn't sure I did, considering the vicious, vicious *thing* I had sensed just beneath.

"I also . . . there's a . . ." I tapped my breastbone.

"It's all right," he said. "That's just your wolf."

"I didn't lose my soul, but I gained a wolf?"

"A werewolf is dual-natured. Human and wolf."

"She smelled meat, blood." *Bloody meat.* "She wanted it."

"She got it. Now she can be at peace."

She didn't feel at peace. Another tidbit I should probably keep to myself.

"Most packs set that wolf free. They want to kill. They thrive on destruction."

"And your pack is different because of you."

"For the most part, yes."

"The most part? What does that mean?"

"I can calm the wolf, but I can't make it go away." Gideon twitched one shoulder, and the skin moved in a different direction from the bones, the movement more wolf than man, emphasizing his words. The wolf was always within.

Waiting.

"Can that wolf get out?" How vigilant did I have to be to keep from becoming what Ash would insist I already was—a vicious, murdering serial killer of a beast?

"If you want her to."

"But—"

"I'm the alpha, but I'm not God."

"You're their god."

He shook his head, and that hair he hadn't had swirled over his shoulders—captivating, enticing. I had to drag my eyes away.

"I'm their leader, and if they choose to give allegiance, to allow me to tame their beast, they are tamed. If they choose not to, they are not pack. Or at least not *my* pack."

"Wouldn't that make them lone wolves?"

"Unless someone gave them a chance. Werewolf packs aren't known for their generosity."

Yet Badru, the worst of the worst according to many, had taken one in. I had to wonder about that.

"The two packs are one now, right?" Though I didn't think Zane had gotten the memo.

"Close. Maybe." He threw up his hands. "I know better than to think everyone is going to accept a completely new way of life. Badru's pack has lived with their wolf both vicious and free for quite a while."

"And they agreed to give that up?"

"If I'd lost, my wolves would have given up *their* way of life. A strong pack makes everyone safer. And a strong pack comes from a solid pack structure, an alpha and a luna; their combined magic holds them as one."

"I'm not magic."

"You are. It might take some time to discover how." Gideon came closer, but he didn't touch me, and for that I was grateful. "I promised you nothing would ever keep us apart."

His expression was the same one he'd worn the last time he'd said those words, and because of that, because of all we'd both said, all we'd both lost, my voice was broken, hoarse. "But it did."

"You thought I ran off and never thought of you again?"

"Everyone thought you ran off, even your parents."

"Did *you?*"

"I thought you were dead, Gideon." I spread my hands. "I mean, you had to be. Not a word, not a whisper, not a trace of you was ever found. Forgive me for not considering you might be a werewolf."

"Sarcasm is a new side to you."

"I have a lot of new sides."

"I'll look forward to uncovering them."

He wasn't uncovering anything if I had my way.

"Why did you choose me?"

"You know why."

"I don't. I—"

His patience snapped with a nearly audible *ping*. "I needed a mate. There's power in two that there can never be in one."

"All right. I get that."

Tell me, I thought. *Tell me you love me, that you never got over me. That she meant nothing. That always, forever, there was, is, there will only be me.*

"Despite what the hunter believes, we aren't all vicious, evil, soulless killing machines capable of every vice and sin known to man and beast."

"Okay, but wh—"

"Because we don't *do* incest."

My gaze flew his.

THE STRANGER FROM
ACROSS THE TRACKS

"*I* can count, Sarah, and so could everyone else, which did explain the hasty wedding."

"You don't . . . you can't . . . She *could* be—"

"She isn't."

"How can you be so sure?"

"Because Patrick liked guys."

I hadn't thought my eyes could go any wider, but they did. I'd been under the impression no one had known the truth about Patrick back then but Patrick and me. Later his family, Frankie, a few others. In retrospect, probably too many to keep the secret forever, but as no one had blazed it across every news outlet far and wide, I didn't think that information was common knowledge.

How had Gideon discovered it?

"I was jealous." Gideon glanced down and away. "You two were so close, you finished each other's sentences half the time, and I was the stranger from across the tracks."

"That's not—"

"It is true." He drew in a breath, and as he let it out, his head, his gaze slowly lifted. "Or it was. Your friendship with him bothered me. Shouldn't have, but I was a dumb kid in a whole lot of ways."

He still resembled that kid in a lot of ways too, and it was hard for my brain to see, hear, understand that duality.

"I confronted Patrick. Not sure what I planned to do or say after that. Punch him in the nose?" He gave a laugh-snort. "But he saw that I was miserable, scared, and he understood miserable and scared better than a lot of people, so he told me."

"He trusted you with that secret?"

"As he pointed out, he trusted me with you, and to Patrick, you were as precious to him as any secret."

My eyes stung. Patrick had been my best friend, my companion for over half my life. It would be overly dramatic to say he'd saved my life and Jenna's, but he *had* given us a life, and it had been a good one. There hadn't been a day since I'd lost him that I hadn't felt his loss as a physical pain. I'd wanted it to fade so badly, and today, for a while, it had. All I'd needed was the moon to call my name.

"He—he—never told me that."

"Why would he?" Gideon shrugged his wolf-shrug. "I was dead, right?"

"Right. You had no reason to be jealous." I didn't bother to add the thought that drifted through my brain.

All I ever wanted was you.

Since the day Gideon had disappeared, I'd believed in my head, my heart, that I would love him until the end of time. If he was dead, I didn't have to stop. I could love the gilded image of the boy he'd been for always.

Now Gideon was back, and while he might look like a boy in some ways on the outside, on the inside he wasn't any longer. There were times I wanted to throw myself into his arms and never let him go, but I also wanted to tear him into itty-bitty pieces with my teeth.

How was that for a dual nature?

"I was a kid," Gideon repeated. "You were my everything."

And you were mine.

His words, my thoughts—past tense.

"Why didn't you let me know you were all right?"

"I wasn't."

The two words murmured just above a whisper fell into a silence so deep it echoed.

"There was no one to nose-bump you," I said.

"I didn't have control of my wolf, and I couldn't come back to you like that. Like that, I didn't want to. By the time I did, by the time I could . . . you were married, and I saw that you'd be better off with him."

Had I been? I didn't know.

"Think about it. If I'd shown up at your door, what would you have done?"

"Stopped crying."

His lips tightened. I waited for him to say he was sorry, but he didn't.

"I was a no one with nothing even before I was changed."

"You weren't no one to me. And how can you have nothing if you have love?"

He rolled his eyes, and the now familiar urge to punch him washed over me.

"You'd have walked away from Patrick, followed me into an uncertain future where I had no job, no home, no true understanding of what was to come?"

"Yes," I said, but he kept speaking right over me.

"And your baby?"

"Our baby."

He frowned, obviously annoyed by my comment. He'd been in the zone.

"Jenna is *our* child, remember?"

"How could I forget? That's the reason this is happening."

"What's this?"

"You changed. Us mated. I never wanted it to come to this."

"You didn't want to be married to me?"

"Married and mated are two very different things."

"Why?"

"Two humans marry, two wolves are mated."

"Gotcha. And what do two werewolves do?"

"If they're the alpha and the luna, they produce an heir to secure the future of their pack."

"About that—" I began, but he carried on right over me for a second time.

"Without one, I'm considered weak. Constant challenges will follow, and sooner or later, I'll lose."

The back of my neck prickled. "And then?"

"My magic and my pack are absorbed by the victor." He paused, his expression stark, almost hopeless. "My mate is either taken as a mate by the winner or killed."

"Okay," I said, though it was *not* okay. "But you have an heir. You have Jenna. Doesn't that solve your problem?"

His gaze met mine. "Only if she's a wolf."

"Oh, hell no." I hadn't become what I had only to have my daughter changed anyway.

"I want you to take her out of here."

The idea of going back to the "real" world gave me the heebie-jeebies. I wasn't sure I was ready. What if I lost control? What if I killed someone? What if I left, and when I came back, Gideon was gone again?

"You're the alpha. Why don't you just send her?"

"I'm not her alpha, and she won't go without you."

I wasn't so sure of that.

He strode to the door, opened it. "Bring me the girl. Jenna. As soon as she returns."

Something large and hulking moved off down the hall.

"Lay this out for me," I said as Gideon returned. "I take Jenna back to the UW, pat her on the head, tell her everything's fine, and then . . .?"

"Tell everyone else the same."

"And where was Jenna when I lost my mind and sent for the FBI?" I hadn't gotten the FBI, but that wasn't the point.

"She went on a field trip with Dr. Maldonado."

"The mad scientist who's no longer with us? How are we gonna explain a dead professor?"

"Dr. Maldonado isn't dead. She's just no longer with us."

She? Huh. Why had I assumed Dr. Danny was male? No idea, but I was glad I didn't have to confront, report, kill the professor I'd thought was having an inappropriate relationship with my girl. One less thing.

"Maldonado's back in her lab," Gideon continued. "And she's told everyone that she and Jenna took a field trip."

"What the fucking fuck?"

"When did you start cursing?"

"In childbirth," I said shortly. "Explain why Maldonado has slipped a gear and made up a BS story."

"I told her to."

"You . . . what?"

"Badru hired her to cure the virus. Badru was an asshole of the first order. Dr. Maldonado learned not to cross said asshole. I am now—"

"The new asshole," I interrupted, and he scowled.

"If I say jump, Dr. Maldonado jumps because she still believes the threat of death for disobedience imposed by Badru, but also because I'm the one now funding her research." Gideon twitched one shoulder. "Badru was rich."

"Pillaging for centuries must be pretty lucrative. Why'd he even bother to start a werewolf women trafficking ring?"

"Because he could."

"And now you inherit his pack, his money, his magic?"

Gideon spread his hands. He appeared embarrassed.

"Wait . . . what was his magic?"

"He could bring the storm. Among other things."

"If to the victor go mountains of spoils, why aren't were-wolves killing one another right and left?"

"Because the punishment for killing another wolf, outside of a challenge to the alpha, fought in a ring, is death. Without that law, we'd wipe ourselves out. There'd be no more pack and—"

I held up a hand before he said, yet again, *Pack is everything.* "Got it."

Gideon quickly briefed me on the remainder of the story Maldonado had agreed to. It made sense.

"Okay," I said. "I'll take Jenna back, but . . ."

Gideon tilted his head, the movement so canine I stifled a wince.

"Before we go, don't you want to tell her the truth?"

How many times had I dreamed of Gideon returning, of him meeting his daughter, of us all living in happily ever after land?

Far too many.

"It's not that I don't want to," Gideon said. "It's that we shouldn't. The more who know the secret, the less chance there is of keeping it. There are those that would kill her so she couldn't become an heir and those that would kill her so she would."

I worried my bottom lip. "We'll need to keep an eye on Zane. He's up to something."

Gideon's amber eyes went topaz. Had my eyes taken on a jeweled tone—blue become aquamarine or perhaps cerulean—to complement my elevation to shape-shifter royalty? I needed a mirror.

"No doubt. But Zane wouldn't dare make a move," Gideon said. "Not yet."

"Have you met Zane?"

He didn't laugh. *Did* he laugh?

"We need to deal with the issue of your hunter."

"He's not mine."

Gideon turned away. "That's not what it looked like."

The kiss. Right. How could I have forgotten? It had been a memorable kiss. Was that because Ash's kiss was truly awesome or because I'd hadn't had anyone's tongue in my mouth or vice versa since—

"I haven't slept with him."

Why did I say that? At least I kept the thought that followed it —*I haven't slept with anyone*—inside my head.

Gideon considered me. "Sex isn't the only thing that creates an unbreakable bond."

True. There was friendship, shared dreams, shared lives, shared danger. I knew that better than anyone.

"Let him go."

I'd wondered if Gideon could laugh. I had my answer when he did, for far longer than I thought was necessary, considering.

"I'm serious."

Gideon managed to rein in his amusement. "I vowed to let Zane deal with the hunter."

"Why?"

"Why do you think?"

I didn't have to think; I knew. "Because he killed Zane's family."

We had the Hatfields and the McCoys. The Capulets and the Montagues. The hunters and the hunted.

Except which one was which?

"Then Zane killed Ash's family right back."

"The hunter started it."

My eyebrows lifted at the childish response. "I'm happy to swap clichés. Two wrongs don't make a right."

"Right. Wrong. We're past that. If I let the hunter go, there'll be rebellion. I promised Zane."

"Screw Zane!"

"I need to appease him at the moment. He's dangerous."

"Then kill him."

It occurred to me that I was proposing Gideon do to Zane what I was asking him *not* to let Zane do to Ash. I never said I was logical. I was also a lot more okay with killing than I'd been yesterday.

"He's the highest-ranking wolf from Badru's pack. There are those that would still follow him if he asked. We need to become one unbreakable, unbendable, undividable unit before I do anything about him."

"When we ran, we seemed like one pack to me."

"Did you see Zane?" Gideon asked.

I shook my head. I had noticed his absence, and it had bothered me.

"A few of Badru's wolves ran with Zane elsewhere. They'll come around once they see that being a member of our pack is the safest choice. If I cause a rift too soon, that rift could tear us apart. After all I've done to get here, I'm not letting that happen."

"Did you nose-bump Zane?"

Gideon shook his head. "If I didn't create them, they have to agree."

"Agree? You're the king. *Their* king. You're magic, for Christ's sake! *Make* them!"

"I . . . I can't. Like I said, the wolf is always within, and unless you agree to keep it there, even magic won't."

Before I could argue or ask anything more, someone knocked.

"Come," Gideon ordered.

Jenna stepped inside. Her gaze went first to me, and I smiled. Must not have been very convincing because she frowned, crossed the room, and took my hand before she addressed Gideon. "It's done."

How could I have forgotten she'd left to save more girls?

"And they are—" Gideon began.

"Cured. Just like the ones I injected here."

"You brought them back?"

Jenna nodded, but she didn't appear happy about it. Neither was I.

"Why would you bring them here?"

Jenna's gaze flicked to Gideon, who seemed genuinely puzzled by the question. "Where else would they go?

"Back to their lives?"

"Can you imagine the outcry if dozens of missing women suddenly reappeared? The scrutiny that would bring? The hunters that would come? They'd be killed the same as any one of us. Easier because they're new, uninitiated, babes in a whole new world.

"So you're going to make them mates against their will? Isn't that what you were trying to stop when you challenged Badru?"

"I was trying to stop more from being taken. From now on, in our territory, the only females to join the pack will be those who want to."

"Who would wa—"

He held up a hand. "We can't put the bitten back the way they were. All we can do is save them from an agonizing death."

"Isn't that what Badru had planned when he commissioned the serum?"

Jenna squeezed my hand. "Badru planned to sell those girls to other packs to use however they wanted to. Slaves. Concubines. Baby-making machines."

"With us, they'll have a better life than they would have had with him," Gideon said. "They'll have a say in their futures. They'll have a choice within the confines of our world. I promise."

I looked into his eyes, and for some reason, I trusted him.

Of course, the last time I'd trusted him, I'd wound up pregnant and alone. Still I'd be there to make sure he kept this promise. However . . .

"Those girls were kidnapped; they've been missing. Aren't

there law enforcement agencies searching for them if not other hunters?"

"I'll handle that." Gideon's words, his voice held the finality of a supreme leader unused to anyone questioning him. "Jenna, your mom's going to take you back to school."

I waited for her to say she didn't need me to do that, didn't want me to, steeling myself against the twinge I always got whenever she'd said so in the past.

Instead, she nodded and tugged me toward the door.

"You send cops after us," Gideon said, and Jenna paused, "they'll die. If you send hunters, your mother will."

Our daughter made a soft sound of amusement, then she gave him the finger and hauled me out the door.

ENDS AND MEANS.
ALL THAT NOISE.

*N*o one tried to stop us as we exited the werewolf hostel. Instead, everyone we saw bowed their heads and murmured, "Your Majesty."

It gave me the wiggies.

As we entered the cool cloak of trees, Jenna broke the silence. "Why didn't you tell me that he's my father?"

I stumbled over a stick hidden beneath a sludge of autumn leaves decayed under months and months of winter snow and nearly went down. Would have if Jenna hadn't caught me. She released me almost instantly and stood in my path, eyebrows raised, arms crossed. Classic "I am so peeved" pose.

Night approached on silent feet, tiptoeing across a forest not yet highlighted by a rising moon. I felt her fading call, a call I was tempted to follow, if only to get out of there.

"He . . . uh . . . who?"

Jenna released an impatient huff. "Alpha. *Gideon.*" Jenna put a twist on his name that I hadn't heard since she'd said, "Mom!" when she was twelve and I'd embarrassed her in public for the first time. Hadn't missed it. "He's my father."

My laugh sounded as forced as it was. "Why would you think that?"

"For one thing, he's been watching me."

"He . . . what?"

"Remember all the times I saw the black wolf?"

"It was—"

"Him. Yeah. Once a month, on the night of the full moon, from as long as I can remember until I left for college."

"But you told the therapist you'd imagined it."

"If I'd told her the truth, I never would have gotten out of therapy."

Gideon had been watching over us, or at least over her. I wasn't sure what to think about that.

"Just because you saw . . . because he—"

"A few years ago, I overheard Grandmother and Grandfather talking."

Unease trickled over me. Patrick's parents had been thrilled to have a grandchild, for appearance's sake. They'd gone through the motions, but they hadn't really committed. Same as mine only less judgy. Compared to my parents, Patrick's were downright huggable.

"Grandmother said she'd hoped the two of you could get past *the affair*"—Jenna imitated the perfect enunciation and snooty tone of Patrick's mother perfectly—"but it was obvious *that man* would always be between you."

And *voilà*, as Zane would say, the reason for our chilly relationship revealed. Jenna thought I'd cheated on her father.

"Why didn't you talk to me?"

"I should have. But once I started seeing things, I couldn't unsee them. You didn't love Dad."

"That is absolutely not true. I loved him more than anyone except you."

Or at least anyone alive. Or anyone I'd thought was alive.

Dear God, what a mess.

"I saw how you looked at Alpha." Her lips tightened, then she sighed. "You sure didn't look at Dad that way. Ever. Not once."

I swallowed. I didn't know what to say. Story of my life.

"But I didn't connect the dots—I mean, why would I think Dad wasn't my dad?—until I saw you and Alpha together. After that, I couldn't unsee things. How he speaks, how he moves, his hair, his eyes. He's me, or I'm—" Her voice broke; I felt like scum.

"This doesn't change anything, Jenna."

"It changes everything!" She kicked at the leaf sludge, which left a clump of black goop on the tip of one battered boot.

"It doesn't. You're still Jenna."

"I'm not Jenna Sullivan; I'm Jenna . . ." She scowled and tossed one hand back in the direction we'd come. "Whatever the hell his name was. Is." She lifted her face to the sky. "I don't know."

"His name *is*"—maybe was—"Gideon Moran. You're, legally, a Sullivan." Said so on the birth certificate.

Silence settled over the forest, the trees, as if everyone and everything in the world was listening. The wind rustled; some leaves stirred and the hair on the back of my neck rose. I felt like someone was watching, but there was no one.

"Nothing will ever change how much your father—"

She shot me a narrow glance.

"Patrick was your father in every way it was possible to be a father."

"Except one," Jenna muttered.

"Genetics is the least of it." My neck tingled with the lie. Genetics would be the whole enchilada if anyone else discovered the truth.

Springtime meant renewal. Rebirth. But I couldn't let it mean that for my daughter. For her, I longed for a winter of the soul where certain things remained beneath, in readiness, accessible with some loving care. Most importantly, her memory of the father she adored.

"This doesn't change the most important things. How much

Patrick wanted you, how much he loved you and you loved him. That was real, that was true, and it always will be."

Jenna's fingers curled toward her palms. "Why didn't *you* tell me the truth?"

"I promised your . . . I promised Patrick I wouldn't."

It had seemed an easy bargain then. Gideon was gone, most likely dead, never coming back. So who had it hurt?

From the expression flickering across Jenna's face, it was hurting her.

I touched my daughter's shoulder, and she stepped away. "You're telling me that my father—that *Patrick* wanted you to lie to me?"

The answer, of course, was yes. Patrick *had* wanted me to lie to her about this, about a lot of things. About almost everything. And I had. Ends and means. All that noise.

"I'm sorry," I said.

"Sorry doesn't change it."

"Nothing's gonna change it."

"I know." Jenna breathed in, breathed out. "I knew Dad . . . I mean *Patrick* . . ."

I wanted to snap, "Quit calling him that!" Patrick *was* her dad. He always would be. But that was a conversation for later.

"I knew—*know*—how things were for him."

Unease trickled over me all over again. "What things?"

"How things were, make that *weren't* between you."

"You . . . knew?"

She nodded, kicking at the sludge again.

"Why didn't you say anything?"

"After I'd been such a little bitch to you, I didn't feel like I had any right to bring it up."

"You were wrong. Did your father know?"

She cast me a funny look. "Of course."

Patrick hadn't told me either. Huh.

"I tried to understand it," she continued. "I wanted to, but I never could."

I always thought that if Jenna knew, she *would* understand. I'd tried to get Patrick to tell her everything once she was older, but he held me to my deal. He thought the truth would change things between them. I didn't. Guess I'd been wrong.

Guilt flickered, but I tamped it down. Patrick would have been the first to tell me that guilt changed nothing.

"Times were different then. We made a bargain. My silence, my compliance, my . . ." I spread my hands. "My presence at his side."

The crease between her eyebrows deepened. "In exchange for what?"

I thought it was obvious, but I said it anyway. "Gideon was gone. I waited as long as I could for him to come back, but I was eighteen and pregnant in a small town. So I took the offer of the name Sullivan, a home, a life. But the most important thing was you. You were the glue that kept it all together."

"Kept what together?"

"The myth, the man, the legend of Senator Sullivan. I'd make the same deal again, though Patrick wouldn't have to anymore. Like I said, times were different. Being a gay senator has cachet now."

"Gay . . ." Jenna's eyelashes fluttered the way they always did when she was surprised, and I got a very bad feeling. "Wait . . . What? Dad was . . . Patrick was . . . gay?"

"You said you knew. That he knew!"

"I meant that you didn't love him the way he loved you. Obviously, he knew that."

I straightened as if a stick had poked me in the butt. "I loved him exactly the way he loved me. We were partners. Best friends." My eyes prickled. "I'll miss him; I'll mourn him forever."

"How could you possibly keep a secret like that for so long?"

"We got good at it."

"And now?"

"Now what?"

"Are you going to tell the truth?"

"No." I frowned. "Why would I?"

"Because it's *the truth*."

"I promised to keep the secret, and I will."

"You just told me."

I ignored that. "It's what your father wanted, and it's the least I can do for him."

She seemed to be thinking, maybe agreeing. I wasn't sure.

"What about . . .?" Jenna lifted her chin to indicate the warehouse we could no longer see on the other side of all the trees. "What do you really think he'll do if I tell his secret?"

"He isn't going to kill you, but . . . he'll do something. Pretty much anything for the pack."

Gideon hadn't said this, hadn't needed to. The instant I'd changed I'd felt the same.

"You're pack now. Where does that leave me?"

"Safe." I touched her face, and she let me. "I'll make sure of it."

"I know." Her gaze lowered. "I wish Dad were still alive. I wish that he was really my dad. I wish I didn't know all that I know. But mostly . . ." She lifted her eyes, and they twinkled with unshed tears. "I wish you hadn't had to do what you did to save me."

"It'll be all right."

"Will it? What if someone shoots you again?"

I swallowed and tasted barbequed werewolf. Then I pulled her into my arms, but I didn't say a thing. We both knew the answer to that what-if.

Jenna allowed me to hold her longer than she had since she was too young to get away, which told me more than her words that she was scared. Jenna wasn't a cuddler.

"Mom?" She pulled back, peered into my face. "He needs an heir. Isn't that me?"

157

I considered lying, but she needed to know.

"You're only the heir if you're changed." I resisted the sudden and nearly uncontrollable urge to bare my teeth and growl. "That ain't gonna happen."

"But—"

"I'll figure something out."

What I'd figured out so far was that I needed to lie again. At forty-one I should be, theoretically, capable of bearing a child. And that was what I'd let Gideon and everyone else believe for as long as I could.

"You need to—"

"Keep my mouth shut." Jenna extricated herself from my arms. "Duh."

There she was. My mini-me.

We walked on in silence until we reached the outskirts of Lunar Lake. Full dark had fallen; the moon shimmered across the surface of the water. Mesmerizing.

I didn't realize I'd stopped walking, taken up staring, until Jenna grabbed my arm and tugged. "Someone's gonna see you mooning at the moon and call Uncle Joe."

I tugged my gaze from the captivating, lustrous glow. "That would not be good."

"You're gonna have to tell him something. Frankie too."

We hurried along the tree line, hugging the shadows as we skirted the lake. Jenna shivered in a bone-chilling spring wind, but not me. First time I'd been happy about my off-kilter body temperature. At least that wind seemed to be keeping the town's residents off the street.

"I'll tell them what you're gonna tell everyone. You went with Dr. Maldonado—"

She held up her hand. "Field trip. I was briefed."

"By who?"

"The chief werewolf minion."

"Zane?"

Jenna let out a soft sound that might have been mistaken for amusement if she hadn't wrinkled her nose the way people did at the scent of a nasty baby diaper. "He wants to be but no. The old guy. Wendell."

"I wonder how long he'll stay chief minion if Zane wants the job."

"Wendell wouldn't have that job if he didn't have skills."

We scooted across Lakeview Drive, then into my yard where we slid through the gloom thrown by the house until we reached the garage. I used the code on the door, then climbed behind the wheel of my Volvo SUV and started the engine.

Jenna picked the key fob from the cupholder where I always left it. "Sooner or later, someone's gonna steal your car if you keep leaving this in it."

If the first car thief to enter Lunar Lake in . . . forever, as far as I knew, got past the garage door code, they were gonna steal the thing anyway. An old argument, one I didn't bother to voice.

I glanced into the rearview mirror and paused, captured by the brand-new shade of my eyes. "Cerulean." I could also swear my hair had streaks of moonstone. "Why didn't you tell me?"

"That's nothing compared to the aquamarine they flare when you're super pissed or when you're a wolf. I'm jealous."

I put the car into gear. "Don't be."

I couldn't even admire them then. What wolf had a mirror?

"How does everyone explain brand new eye colors?"

"Only royalty have jewel-toned eyes." Jenna shrugged. "Everyone else probably says they got contacts."

We were out of town in seconds, and I picked up the conversation right where we'd left off. An uncommon occurrence lately when a dropped conversational ball would have rolled under my couch to eat lint forever before I remembered where my brain had been.

Was my mind clicking along better since the change, or was the barrage of heightened emotions—fear, joy, anger, agony—

causing heightened clarity? Either way, I'd take what I could get for as long as I could get it.

"What sort of skills does Wendell have that might keep someone like Zane in his place?"

"Got me. All I know is that Wendell is slavishly devoted to his alpha."

"Isn't that what *beta* means?"

"Meh." She waggled her hand. "The story I heard is that Wendell was changed by this horrible, bitch of a werewolf queen."

"Isn't that redundant?"

Jenna cast me a glance. "Glass houses, Mom."

I snorted. "Go on."

"She liked to bathe in the blood of her servant girls after she'd tortured them a while. She was kind of a sadist."

"Kind of?"

"Wendell tried to stop her. Wound up as a minion. More torture and so on."

Something tickled my brain. "This sounds like the Blood Countess."

"Right! Elizabeth Báthory. How'd you know?"

"Your father and his Saturday afternoon bad-movie marathons."

"Sheesh, Mom. Why would anyone make a movie about her? She was awful."

"She was also alive in the sixteen hundreds."

Jenna shrugged.

"How old is this guy?"

"You've met him, right?"

I rolled my eyes. "The Blood Countess was a vampire."

"Not."

"A possible inspiration for Dracula."

"Might be why they staked her ass."

"She died in jail." As I recalled, a walled-up prison with small slits only large enough to insert food and water. Though it *had* been a B movie and not a docu-drama.

"Nope. They staked her, threw her in an unmarked grave. As they'd neglected to stake her with silver, she crawled out, eventually showed up here."

"Here?" My high-pitched question bounced off the enclosed interior of the car.

"Well, not *right* here. She went back to bathing in blood, first the Native Americans. Gave rise to some scary legends. Then she took out quite a few settlers."

"Let me guess, they blamed the Native Americans."

Jenna shot me with her forefinger. "Got it in one. Then it was the poor, the insane, the homeless."

"And then?"

"Then Alpha killed her, and now Wendell is his slave instead."

There was more to that story, a lot more, but I wasn't sure I wanted to hear it, considering.

It didn't escape my notice that she did not use Gideon's name but continued to refer to him as Alpha. Which was, at least, several steps above *that asshole who got you pregnant.*

"Wendell will do anything to keep his alpha in power."

"Won't they all?"

"Not sure about Zane. He might have been a good beta for Badru who was basically a serial killer, but I don't trust him."

"Neither do I."

"Wendell's different. Before he won the battle, Alpha had to contend with a lot of unrest. You know how guys are when they don't get any for a long time?"

I blinked. "Uh . . ."

"If they don't have sex, they get pissy. No females equals no sex." The shoulder closest to me twitched upward. "For the most part. Sure, there are human women, but it's not the same."

"Because?"

"Wolves mate for life. That's all the explanation I got. Not that werewolves and humans don't have sex, but it's not the same, and it's frowned upon. Both men and wolves who don't get any start arguments, bump chests."

I'd had no idea.

"There were little revolts all over the place. Wendell's good at sneaking around, ferreting out plots and schemes. If Alpha knows about the unrest, he can squash it before it happens."

Did I want to know how Gideon *squashed* things? Nope.

"A beta that will lay down their life for the alpha is . . . what's that saying? 'A worth far above rubies.'"

"Shakespeare?" That Renaissance literature course she'd taken for her English elective was paying off.

"Proverbs."

It took me a second to connect the word with— "The *Bible?*"

"You'd be surprised what you hear around werewolves. One of the big guys—"

"Cro-Magnon heads?"

She laughed. "Yeah. One of them fought in the Crusades."

"Where the Christians"—using the term loosely—"attempted to wipe out the Infidel."

"A.k.a. the Muslims."

"I have a feeling quite a few of the crusaders met a *Qutrub* and came back furry."

"You get what you pay for."

"Karma?"

"Sometimes it happens," Jenna said.

I had not found this to be the case.

"So werewolves live forever?"

"Barring an unfortunate encounter with silver."

"Or a virus."

"Right."

It was handy to have a daughter who knew the ins and outs of the werewolf world I'd been tossed into. Now all I had to do was get her out of it.

We reached campus, and I coasted to the curb in front of her apartment. "I don't want you being the on-call vaccinator for trafficked werewolf women."

"Say that five times fast."

"I'll say it as many times as I have to for you to hear me."

"But—"

"What if you get bitten?"

"Daddy-o can nose-bump them, remember? They'll be gentle as lambs."

"Will they?" I remembered the pain I'd felt, the madness that had threatened.

She knew where my mind had gone. I'd never had a poker face.

"What happened to you, how fast you changed, how quickly the virus hit you . . . that was weird. He said it was because you're the luna."

"He should know. But I'm not willing to take the chance of your being bitten. I became this to avoid that. So, please, please stay away from anything werewolf. Let the mad scientist handle it."

In the past, ordering Jenna to do anything usually resulted in her doing it.

Instead, she nodded. "All right."

I frowned. That had been far too easy. "Jenna, I mea—"

"You need to watch Zane. He's gunning for alpha, and if he manages it—"

"I'm dead. I was briefed."

I'd hoped she would laugh, or at least smile, at my use of her earlier terminology. Sadly, my daughter didn't seem to notice my cleverness any more today than she had in the past ten years.

"Why aren't you worried?" she asked.

"If it comes to a challenge, I think Gideon can take him."

"But what if—"

"If you let life be about the what-ifs, you never live the right now."

"Who are you, and what have you done with my mother?"

I set my hand atop hers atop her knee. "I'm still your mother, but I'm the luna now, and I'm going to have to live in that world."

Jenna looked down and whispered, "I'm sorry."

"It's not your fault, and it's okay."

"Is it?"

"Yes," I said, surprised to discover it was. "I've been what-iffing since Gideon disappeared. What if he hadn't? What would our life be like? I'm going to find out. Who gets a second chance like this?" Even if I was getting it as a werewolf.

But first, I had to get over twenty-plus years of anger at him for leaving, disappearing, dying because none of that had been true. Still, old habits.

I reached past her and opened the glove compartment where I'd stashed her phone. She snatched it as if it was her long-lost pacifier.

"You can"—I made the international sign of the cell phone—thumb to my ear, pinky to my lips—"whenever. I'll answer."

"Okay." Jenna hugged me and was gone quicker than any bunny out of the car and into her apartment building.

Of course, I wasn't sure I would be able to answer whenever. If I was running around the forest on four paws, I wouldn't be carrying a cell phone.

A LONG TIME AGO IN A DISTANT FORGOTTEN WORLD

"*W*here the hell have you been?"

I *eeped* at the voice that greeted me as I stepped into my darkened house less than an hour later. The big-ass hat on the head of the man silhouetted in the moon's glow through the front window revealed the speaker's identity if his voice already hadn't. I needed to get back the key Patrick had given his brother for emergencies.

I flicked on the lights. Joe looked ready to explode.

My phone began to ring. I cast a quick glance at the caller ID —Frankie—then winced apologetically as I answered. I held up one finger, and Joe's face and neck went from mottled red to completely scarlet.

"Where the hell have you been?"

Same question, different man. Except Frankie didn't shout; Frankie never shouted. Nevertheless, I thought he might explode too.

"I found Jenna."

The truth in that simple sentence stopped them cold. It also answered, albeit vaguely, their question. Two birds, one stone. Gotta love it.

"Where was she?" Frankie asked an instant before Joe asked the same.

Stereo interrogation. Awesome.

"Field trip."

"A what?" Joe shouted.

The derisive exhale from the other end of the line revealed Frankie had deduced my brother-in-law was there without my having to waste time telling him.

"She went into the field with a professor to help with an experiment." This was also true, or near enough to sound plausible. "Jenna's twenty-three years old. She didn't think she needed to tell anyone."

"She thought wrong," Joe muttered.

Frankie didn't comment. I hoped he was buying this.

"They were only supposed to be there a day or two, but their SUV got stuck in the ass-end of nowhere, and they ended up sleeping in it for a few nights."

"A few?" Joe was still shouting. "And they couldn't phone home?"

"Jenna didn't have her phone."

Trust Frankie to remember the details.

"And considering this is Jenna we're talking about, how'd that happen?"

"The vet school student who was supposed to help got sick, and the prof asked Jenna to fill in last minute. She was excited to be asked, considering she's an undergrad, and she forgot a few things."

"Forgot," Frankie repeated, skepticism dripping from the word.

"I find it hard to—" Joe began.

"Even if she had remembered her phone," I interrupted, "they were ten miles from Gettysville." A town notorious for having the shittiest, sometimes nonexistent cell phone service for every carrier for miles in every direction.

Both Frankie and Joe went silent, and I jumped in with the rest of the story Gideon had fed us.

"They finally managed to wave down one of the Amish and rode in his buggy to the Gettysville General Store, which has a landline. They called me, and I went to get them."

The addition of the Amish buggy was a nice touch, added some hours to the timeline and could be used to gloss over the holes in my own. I'd disappeared yesterday, though maybe, if I was lucky, no one had noticed right away.

That seemed to be the case since neither Joe nor Frankie mentioned it.

"Why didn't she tell her roommate?" Frankie asked.

"Yeah," Joe agreed. "She didn't think an FTA would cause us to put out an APB?"

My brain quickly translated Joe-speak into *failure to appear* and *all-points bulletin.*

"Like I said, she jumped at this chance. You know how she is about wolves."

I received acknowledgment to that statement, also in stereo.

"All right." Joe adjusted the brim of his *Longmire* hat and headed for the door. "I need to call off the dogs on both Jenna and—" Joe turned. "What about that girl?"

"Yeah," Frankie said in my ear. "What about that girl?"

I rubbed my forehead. The girl was ashes, and no one had thought to include her in the briefing.

"What girl?" I asked, still buying time as I lowered my hand.

"What girl?" both Joe and Frankie repeated in a robotic monotone.

Joe stared out the window. I could hear Frankie breathing. The questions that should have followed did not. Something was weird here. I continued with my lies just to see where they led.

"I'm going to visit a friend for a few weeks."

"You don't have—" Frankie began at the same time Joe said, "What fr—?"

I touched my forehead again and repeated the semi-lie. Gideon could be a friend. If I let him.

"You're going to visit a friend," they agreed in the same flat tone, neither one asking the name of the mythical friend they both knew I didn't have.

I'd stumbled over my magic power. Touch my forehead, make a suggestion, people believed whatever I said. The question was, would they *do* whatever I said as well? I decided to find out.

"Could you let your mother know, Joe?"

"Sure thing. Have a nice visit!" Joe exited stage left.

I waited for Frankie to sign off too. Instead, he threw another wrench my way. "Have you seen Ash?"

"Who's Ash?"

And just like before, Frankie repeated, "Who's Ash?"

"Okay, then, talk to you soon!" I said brightly, and Frankie responded, "Talk to you soon!"

The line went dead, and I pocketed the phone, then climbed two flights of stairs so I could stare out my dormer window at the lake and think about what had just happened. People believed what I said; they did what I said too. Would this power work on werewolves too? Gideon's magic had.

So many things I needed to learn.

I turned away from the view that had given me so much comfort in the past but was not doing a thing for me today. Maybe because today what I'd often needed comfort for—the loss of Gideon Moran—no longer existed. I still felt adrift.

Who was he now? Who was I? And how would we fit back together? *Could* we fit back together?

I packed a duffel, stuffed my laptop into its case, and threw everything into my car. Within minutes, I'd returned to the warehouse. The blast-proof door gaped open.

I stepped inside. "Hello?" My voice echoed in the empty space.

The cages were gone. No chains. No keys. The only hints that there'd been a werewolf rumble were the few tufts of fur—both black and silver—resembling tiny tumbleweeds as they rolled across the blood-spattered floor.

In the hall, I hesitated. Left to the dungeon, right to the lair. Decisions, decisions.

I took a left, then navigated the twisty, turn-y route to the cell. The door gaped open. The damp, dark area loomed empty too.

"Looking for someone?"

I gasped, spun.

Gideon.

He leaned against the wall, tousled hair tumbling over bare shoulders. The top button of his jeans gaped open, revealing the familiar beginnings of a happy trail from his navel to his—

I forced my gaze upward as memories of my exploration of said trail flickered and flashed. "Do you ever wear a shirt? It's not even forty degrees outside."

He gave a wolf-shrug, and I had to close my eyes for a second. He was both the same and so very, very different.

"You'll discover you run hot."

I've been running hot for a year now, I thought, and then had to turn my laugh, cry, chortle—one or all of them—into a cough. My specialty. At least he didn't seem to notice.

"The more time you spend without clothes, the more restrictive they feel when you're in them. Be happy I put on pants."

I was not going to discuss, or think about, that. Instead, I threw out my hand to indicate the empty cell. "What did you do with him?"

"By *him*, you mean the murderous hunter?"

"Pot. Kettle."

Gideon's eyes flared topaz, but he didn't take the bait. "He's been moved to a secure location."

"*What* secure location?"

He didn't answer, so I gave my new magic power a whirl. Maybe I could discover things I needed to know as well as erase them. I lifted my fingertips to my forehead, rubbing as if he'd made my head hurt, which he had. "What secure location?"

Nothing happened. No *ping*, no spilling of the beans. WTH?

Instead, Gideon straightened away from the wall, muscles flexing in the six-pack he hadn't had at eighteen. "Wendell?"

The beta materialized at Gideon's elbow so fast he had to have been waiting just out of sight around the corner. "I've found a way to remove blood stains from concrete, Alpha. I wish I'd had hydrogen peroxide back when . . ." He stared into the air, perhaps into the past.

I got it. Back when he'd been cleaning up blood for the Blood Countess, hydrogen peroxide would have been really handy.

"Thank you." Gideon set a hand on the old man's shoulder, bringing him back from a place he should definitely leave behind. "I don't know what I'd do without you. Can you stow our things in the luna's car?"

"Immediately, Alpha." I waited for him to click his heels, maybe salute; instead, he scurried off.

"Must be nice to have a minion."

"It is."

"I heard what you did for him."

Gideon looked away and said nothing.

"You hated it when anyone got picked on."

His laugh held not a trace of amusement. "Picked on as a new euphemism for torture. You still have a way with words."

He was deflecting, same as he always had.

"You always stood up for the little guy, even if you ended up at the walk-in clinic, in detention, or suspended."

"That was a long time ago, in a distant, forgotten world." He jabbed a finger toward the floor. "This world, the werewolf world, is different. Everyone and everything is going to be different, Sarah, including you."

"If things are so different, if *you're* so different, then why *did* you risk your neck to save someone you'd just met?"

"Because Wendell worships me."

"He . . ." I blinked. "What?"

"An alpha needs a beta he can trust completely."

"Zane doesn't seem too trustworthy."

"Zane is not my beta."

He had me there.

"What about the girls? You risked your life for them too."

"And why do you think that was?"

"Because they'd been kidnapped, changed against their will, trafficked. Because what happened to them is wrong."

Gideon twitched one smooth, bare, perfect shoulder. "I've seen worse."

Sympathy fluttered, but I managed to keep from asking what it had been. My brain was already close to exploding outward like an overstuffed suitcase on a Saturday morning cartoon, spewing all the horrible that had been stuffed in it all over the place.

"Then why did you do it?" I asked.

"I saved them too."

I stared at him with narrowed eyes as the dots slowly connected. "So they'd . . . *worship* you? You've been smoking crack if you think I'm going to share you with them."

I didn't plan to partake, but he didn't know that.

Amusement flickered. "Why would you immediately jump to that conclusion? We're wolves. We don't do harems."

"You lost me."

"Wolves mate for life, Sarah. One male. One female."

"All right."

"We mated."

I made a face. "Do you have to call it that?"

He ignored me. "We had a child. That bond is forever."

"Except for the time you had that other mate."

"You think I should have lived alone all these years?" Gideon asked.

"You had a pack; you weren't alone." I certainly hadn't had a pack.

"Pack is everything, but an alpha needs an heir to prove his strength."

"Henry the Eighth much?"

He cast me an annoyed glance. "It is what it is. There are rules in our world, written in the—"

I held up a hand. "*Book of Books.* I remember. You know this whole thing is misogynistic to the nth degree."

"The *Qutrub* is an ancient being, born from ancient magic, from the sands of an ancient world, and ruled by ancient beliefs."

"Got that right," I said.

"To continue to rule, to keep my pack safe, I desperately needed an heir, and that was why I agreed to a mate."

It nearly slipped out of my mouth that he *still* needed an heir, which was the entire reason I was now a luna werewolf queen, but I didn't want to open that kettle of worms. Ever.

I'd lived on the outskirts of a world where information was both currency and power. Politics. What a shit show. But because of it, I knew that some things were best kept to myself.

Wendell reappeared, gave a fussy half-bow. "Everything's ready, Alpha."

"Thank you." Gideon held out a hand, and Wendell placed a T-shirt into it before he executed a military turn and marched away.

"Where is everyone?"

"Those who can went back to the human lives we've created. Did you think we lived in an abandoned warehouse?"

Truthfully, I hadn't thought of it. Too busy becoming a werewolf.

"Under the full moon, we must change, and we must run." Gideon's head appeared through the neck of his bright-white, one-size-too-small T-shirt. You'd think if clothes felt constrictive, he'd wear a shirt two sizes *larger*. I planned to. "But every other night, every other day we live other lives."

"Werewolves go back to their human families?"

"No."

"Why not?"

"Humans age. We don't. The truth comes out eventually, then bad things happen."

"What type of bad things?"

Gideon didn't answer. He didn't have to. I had no problem imagining our heads on silver pikes.

"And the girls?"

"Don't worry about the girls." He strode toward the exit, and I had to hustle to keep up. I could smell the hydrogen peroxide, but the floor was immaculate. You'd never know there'd been a werewolf rumble.

"But I do worry about them. What kind of lives will they have now?"

"Any kind they want to."

"Except the ones they wanted before."

He sighed. I was exasperating. Call it a gift.

"I promise they'll be happy."

Gideon seemed sincere, but what did I know of sincerity anymore? Bottom line? The girls were werewolves; so was I. There was no going back, so we'd have to move forward and make the best of whatever came.

Gideon pushed open the blast-proof door, a staying palm turned in my direction. He looked both ways, sniffed the air, listened, then ushered me forward.

"Can you smell and hear and see better than the average human?" I certainly couldn't.

"No." He allowed the heavy door to close; the lock clicked home. "When we're human—"

"We're human," I finished. "But not really because we have the ability to become a wolf."

As well as our magical superpowers.

Gideon opened the passenger door. "Deep down, we are two-natured, on the surface, we are what we are, when we are."

"Jesus," I muttered as I climbed in. "You're makin' me crazy."

I received another exasperated glance before he slammed the passenger door.

The moon that had risen in the east was making its path to the west. I'd never really noticed how the moon rose in an almost exact arc to the setting sun. Now it called me, and I noticed everything.

Gideon plopped behind the wheel, and I reluctantly pulled my attention from the moon. She was so damn pretty.

"We might not hear and see and smell better," Gideon continued, "but using the senses we do have in more evolved ways can save us nine times out of ten."

"Evolved sounds wolfy to me."

His lips tightened and released along with his breath. "By being aware of what's around us, by visualizing what could happen, by paying attention, always, we can determine what's coming before it comes and meet it, maybe defeat it rather than being surprised."

From his expression as he shifted into drive and steered my car onto the road, he was thinking of other times he'd been surprised. Or, perhaps, that one time. The first time. The last time he'd been completely human.

"How did it happen?"

"Which *it* are you asking about?"

"The big it. The life-changing, *Wow, I'm a werewolf* it."

The rumble of the car's engine filled the silence, reminding me this was *my* car and I'd taken the shotgun seat without a second thought. How unlike me.

"I had a fight with my parents," Gideon said. "I decided to walk to your house. The full moon shone down like ice from the heavens, and it was cold as hell. I cut through the forest. Heard something whimpering. Followed the sound. Shoved aside some brush and—"

"The big bad wolf got you."

"Nope. The whimpering pup. Little bastard."

I checked to see if he was kidding. He wasn't.

"You were changed into a werewolf by a puppy?"

He flicked a glance my way. "No. The pup was the distraction."

"Help me find my puppy near the violent psych ward," I murmured, one of the litany of fears I'd had for Jenna.

"Close enough. I didn't know it was a wolf. I definitely didn't consider it might be a werewolf. Little guy took off. I followed and—"

"*Then* the big bad wolf"—*Emir*—"got you."

"You always wanted a puppy."

"Oh, Gideon. You were bitten trying to bring me a gift? I don't know what to say."

"There isn't anything *to* say. What's done is done. What's past is past."

Silence settled over us. I couldn't stand it.

"What do you do?" Gideon flicked me a quick, confused glance, and I continued. "I mean, other than battle to the death in werewolf rumbles and lope around beneath every full moon."

His confusion became annoyance. Funny, or maybe not so much, that I didn't remember ever seeing that expression directed at me from him. Were all memories of first love as gilded as my own?

"I'm going to be dropped into your life soon. I . . . well . . . it would be helpful if I knew something about it."

"I'm an information security analyst."

"Tech stuff? Huh." Should have seen that coming. Even though our high school had owned three Dell computers that only the supergeeks knew how to use, he *had* been one of them.

"What did you imagine I did in the daylight?"

I hadn't imagined anything; I'd thought he was dead. Since I discovered he was alive, I'd been more preoccupied with staying alive myself and keeping my daughter completely and forever human.

"Considering your habit of walking around shirtless"—and his new and improved physique—"I would have guessed Chippendale stripper."

He didn't take that bait.

"I needed an occupation where punching a clock wasn't required. Where no one would notice if I took time off here and there. Where I could work from home because I might have to move my home between one moon and the next."

"Why would you have to do that?"

"Because a neighbor started asking too many questions, maybe someone, somewhere noticed how little I'd aged? Because a hunter caught wind of the pack. Because the alpha told me to."

"Is that why you took over the pack?" He had never liked being told what to do.

"I did what I had to do to be safe."

"You killed."

"Yes. You don't know what you'll do to become predator and not prey until you're prey. I took over the pack because the viciousness of Emir and those he'd made brought danger to all of us. If a neighbor got too nosy, no more neighbor. Then a hunter would come. Kill the hunter, more hunters come."

"Yet you're going to let Zane kill Ash."

"I'm letting Zane decide what to do with Ash. That doesn't mean he'll kill him."

I snorted. "Right."

Gideon shrugged his wolf-shrug.

"You know his grandfather is like the greatest werewolf hunter of all time?"

Gideon nodded.

"You don't think the entire werewolf hunting tribe is going to rain down on us like hellfire if the golden grandson disappears?"

"I think without him there's going to be chaos, at least for a while."

"That doesn't make it okay."

"Doesn't it?"

"No!"

I could tell by the way his shoulders stiffened and his fingers curled around the steering wheel that he wasn't going to see things my way.

Not yet.

Silence settled over us, and while I tried to stay awake, my eyelids kept fluttering, closing, opening, and becoming heavy once more, but I could . . . not . . . do it.

I woke as dawn broke in the east. The sunrise was beautiful, yet it made me a bit sad. I missed the moon.

A sign flashed past: *Shipwreck Bay – Next Exit.*

There were a hundred, two hundred, three—who knew?— small towns, villages, both incorporated and unincorporated in Wisconsin. I'd never heard of this one, though Patrick had always done his best to visit as many as he could. It was one of the things that had made him an exceptional senator. I didn't think Gina Garofolo would try half as hard or be a quarter as good at the job as Patrick had been.

Gideon took the exit, and as we drove through town, Shipwreck Bay awakened. Citizens walked their dogs, jogged, meandered with a cup of coffee. Many cast us curious glances. I waited for Gideon to lift his hand, wave as if he belonged there, but he didn't.

He took a left turn onto a side street. Halfway down the block, a moving van idled in a driveway. Workers hoisted furniture and headed inside, the speed of their journey determined by the weight of their burden.

Gideon parked in front of the traditional blue and white colonial—pillars, center door, symmetrical windows. I immediately imagined an addition on the right, which would change the annoying—to me—boxy silhouette.

"You just moved here?"

"I did." He got out of the car.

Being new in town explained the curiosity and the lack of neighborly waving.

I got out too. "Why?"

My question stopped Gideon halfway around the front of the Volvo. He glanced at the movers, but they were too far away to hear us and too busy shoving a king-sized mattress through a doorway fashioned in the seventeen hundreds when men rarely topped five-eight.

Nevertheless, he turned his back on them and lowered his voice. "A pack's territory ranges from fifty to one hundred miles. I had claimed fifty. Badru had claimed fifty. Now we have one hundred."

"Yay us!" I punched my fist into the air.

Gideon sighed. "If I want to control such an area, it's best to be in the center, so I moved there. There was also the issue of you."

"Me?"

"Not you, specifically, but whoever the prize turned out to be. I could bring her here, introduce her as my wife, start fresh where no one knew us."

"Then your daughter ended up the sacrificial virgin. And really, Gideon, what the hell?"

He set his hand on my shoulder. From afar, the gesture seemed friendly, no doubt. From afar, no one could see his fingers digging into my flesh.

"The Hakim chose based on who would be the most help to the pack going forward. Jenna had been taking care of the injured. She's good at it."

"She told me about the black wolf that watched from the

forest on the nights of the full moon." I held up a hand. "You knew who she was, so why didn't you send her away the instant she arrived with Maldonado?"

"That would only have drawn more attention. Besides, the Hakim was supposed to choose from the trafficked girls."

"But he wasn't required to."

"No." Gideon strode toward the house and I had to scramble to keep up.

Inside, there was so much white it made my eyes burn.

"This place needs a coat of . . ." I considered the foyer. "Snow-rotted mint or maybe . . . creamed pea soup."

Gideon's laugh startled me. It was the laugh of the boy I had loved, not the humorless bark of the alpha werewolf king.

Our gazes met, and I was struck hard by the memory of the first time I'd seen him, maybe because he was staring at me the way he had the first time he'd seen me. Outside the school office, his first day. I'd run into him and dropped all my books. He'd knelt, picked them up, handed them back, all the while looking at me as if he wanted to know me in ways I didn't even know myself.

"You still do that." Gideon took a step toward me. "I wondered."

I took a step toward him too; I couldn't help myself, couldn't remember in that moment why I shouldn't. "Do what?"

"Make up colors." His fingertips brushed mine, and my skin tingled everywhere.

"I don't"—I hooked my forefinger around his—"make up colors."

"The names." His gaze dipped to my mouth, and my breath caught in my chest. "I always—"

"Mr. Malik?"

I hadn't realized that Gideon's head had begun to dip as well until he straightened and turned away, taking his forefinger and his lips away too.

"No," I began even as Gideon said, "That's me."

I nearly blurted, "Since when?" but Gideon cast me a glance in opposition of everything we'd just shared—no longer warm but cold, no longer inviting but silencing.

The mover, whose coverall labeled him *Ned*, hung over the banister that rimmed the upstairs hall. "You wanna show us where you want the beds?"

"Sure." Gideon trotted up the steps, and even if his gaze hadn't told me to stay where I was, I would have as I had no desire to be involved in the placing of the beds.

Movers continued to haul in furniture that looked like it belonged in a college frat house. In the basement, where they kept the keg and the shockingly loud sound system.

Then again, my knowledge of college frats had been shaped by *Animal House*—classic—and *Old School*, which was probably considered a classic by now too.

Regardless, the couch in the living room was made of Naugahyde the shade of pus. If that hadn't convinced me to sit on a box, the scent of days-old beer that wafted in my direction would have.

Footsteps clattered down the stairs, then both Gideon and Ned appeared.

Ned smiled, and I found myself smiling too as he crossed the room, hand outstretched. "Is this your mom?"

THAT'S A GOOD REASON

$\mathcal{N}$ed's hand, large and hard and calloused, pumped mine. My smile had frozen; my body had too.

His mom?

How could I have forgotten that on the outside I appeared forty-something and Gideon didn't? Gideon wouldn't. Ever.

Then Ned's forehead creased. "You seem familiar. Have we met?"

The frozen smile. I tried to make my expression more natural, didn't have any more luck now than I'd had any of the other times I'd tried at the request of this photographer or that PR person, journalist, or campaign manager.

Yes, I'd avoided the spotlight as much as I could, but I'd still been in it enough to be somewhat recognizable as Mrs. Senator Sullivan. The blonde with the smile of ice.

"No." I withdrew my hand from his. "I don't think—"

"This is Sarah." Gideon's hip bumped mine as he settled his arm across my shoulders, and for a fleeting instant, I felt exactly what I'd felt all the other times he'd done that—back in the day. Pressure at the base of my throat, a hint of tears amid a sudden joy, warmth in the cold, light in the darkness, the possibilities of a love so deep it would last until the end of—

"My wife."

Ned's eyes widened. "Your . . . oh. Um, yeah. Great!"

Gideon's fingers tightened, then released, around my upper arm. "I think so."

A warning rumbled just beneath the surface of his voice. The sun cast through the front window and across Ned's forearms, highlighting the hairs as they lifted and swayed right before he shivered.

"Well, thanks for the check and—" Ned flicked two gnarled fingers away from his forehead—an apology, a salute, a good-bye.

As soon as he was out the door, I stepped back. "You think people are going to believe I'm your wife? Look at me."

He let his gaze wander over me, slowly, suggestively, and my body reacted as it always had.

"Stop that." I turned before he saw how he made me want, need, feel.

Remember.

"Stop what?"

I tensed as he approached, jumped when he touched my shoulder and gently turned me around.

"Wanting you?" He brushed my hair from my forehead, and where he touched, I burned. "I can't."

"I'm not your wife," I whispered.

"You're not my mother either."

I winced.

"I couldn't exactly tell him that you're my mate."

"Why'd you have to tell him anything?"

We stood so close that when he drew breath, his chest brushed my own, and my breasts ached as my nipples pebbled. I had to grind my teeth together until they crunched to keep the moan inside.

From the way he stared at me, he heard it anyhow. But he let me inch away. I'm not sure what I would have done if he hadn't.

"At the least telling him you were my wife made him stop trying to remember where he'd seen you."

"Sooner or later, someone's going to." It was only a matter of time.

It occurred to me that I could have given Ned a push with my mind, and he would have believed whatever I told him. I wasn't used to having a magic power. Would I ever be?

"Does it matter?" Gideon asked. "Patrick's dead. Jenna knows the score."

"My mother-in-law—"

"Can suck it."

I started to laugh, then I couldn't stop. I bent at the waist, tried to catch my breath. "This is all so ridiculous."

"What's ridiculous?"

"Gideon, you have to see how this is going to look to everyone. I'm old enough to be your mother."

"But you aren't, and we both know that."

"No one else will."

"I don't give a shit what people think! Why do you?"

Why did I? Like he'd said, Patrick was dead. Jenna knew the score. And everyone else, including my mother-in-law, could suck it.

God, the idea of telling everyone to suck it, of coming back to Lunar Lake married to—

Wait.

"I can't waltz into Lunar Lake with you on my arm and present you as my new husband."

"Why not?"

"You're Gideon Moran. You're dead."

"Not."

"Right, but—"

"I'm *not* Gideon Moran. I'm Hugh Malik."

"Which is why no one seemed to know your name at the warehouse."

He gave me the regal head bop.

"Though no one called you 'Hugh' either."

"They wouldn't dare. I'm the alpha. Hugh is what I'm called in the human world."

"It's gotta get real confusing when there's more than one alpha around."

He cast me a glance. "There aren't two alphas around for very long."

He had a point.

"I assume you have all the appropriate ID and background to be Hugh in the *human world*."

"You think I became an information security analyst because it was so damn interesting?"

"Yes?"

"Well, it can be, but that's not why. The pack needed someone who could put an end to any searches for the missing. Who could—"

"Stop right there."

I thought of all the times I'd begged the chief to do something more, and he'd said, "I've done all I can. Now we just have to wait."

But I couldn't wait.

"You made sure I couldn't find you. How? You hacked into ViCAP? The FBI?"

"Not me personally. Not then."

"And now?"

Gideon lifted one shoulder, an *aw, shucks, you caught me* without words.

This not only explained the complete disappearance of Gideon but also the lack of information found on the dead were-wolf girl who'd stayed in my home.

She still bothered me.

"There was a girl Ash brought to my house. He thought she was Jenna."

Gideon inclined his head.

"Who was she?"

"I don't know. I did look. I'll keep looking."

"Okay." I wasn't going to give up on finding her family and letting them know, if not the truth, at least something to give them closure. Not having it—I eyed Gideon—really sucked swamp water.

"What else do you do?"

"Change names, build new backgrounds, then trickle it through the information highway. You can't live forever looking exactly the same and expect no one to notice."

"What if they do?"

"Time to move on, though your ability to give a little push is going to be pretty damn handy going forward."

"Push?" I tried to keep my face from betraying me, but I'd never been good at it. I should probably practice. Might keep me alive down the road.

"You weren't exactly cagey when you asked me for the secure location of that murdering SOB hunter."

"He's not—" I began, then gave up. To Gideon, Ash was exactly what he'd said, and trying to change his mind was a waste of time and breath. I had better ways to use both. "I can push people to forget, to believe what I say, to do what say, but I can't push them to answer questions they don't want to answer?"

"You probably can. We won't know the extent of your power until you test it."

"I thought I had. On you."

"I felt the push, which is how I knew for sure what you were up to. But your magic won't work on me. I'm the alpha."

"Sheesh." I rolled my eyes. "It's good to be the king."

"*Robin Hood: Men in Tights.*" His smile at the memory of watching the movie on the VCR in my parents' basement brought forth my own. We'd laughed our asses off in between kissing and—

"My power won't work on you, but yours works on me?"

"I didn't say mine would work on you."

I perked up. "It doesn't?"

"No."

"What about everyone else's?"

"The members of a pack cannot use their magic on their alpha or their luna."

"Cannot because you say so or cannot because they . . . cannot?"

"Isn't it the same?"

"Are you that sure of your power over your people that you think those two statements are the same?"

"They're *our* people. *Our* wolves. And yes."

"You're makin' me crazy." That seemed to be a litany lately.

"They can't because it's forbidden."

"And if they do, what happens? Banishment?"

That would explain Zane's sigma status, though it didn't explain what he'd done to cause it, but I had a pretty good idea.

"Perhaps," Gideon said.

"Slap on the paw? Poke them with silver?"

"Perhaps," he repeated.

I threw up my hands, widened my eyes, and he sighed. "It means we'll decide that when it happens. That's what we do."

"Judge, jury, executioner."

"Now you're catching on."

Was he serious? I didn't know anymore.

Gideon glanced up the stairs. "I have things I need to do in my office."

"Names to change, people to disappear?"

He sighed as if exasperated with me. I didn't blame him. I could be a real PITA, especially when I was uncertain. And what could be more uncertain than becoming a luna werewolf queen?

"I'll start unpacking."

Gideon hesitated. "You sure?"

"What else do I have to do?"

His brow creased, and I saw what he would have looked like if he'd aged as I had. I wanted that so badly it scared me.

"What did you do in Lunar Lake?" he asked.

"I raised Jenna; I helped Patrick." Not as much as I should have, could have. "I worked on the house. I enjoyed it; I was good at it."

"You're still you, Sarah. You're still good at it."

My gaze flicked to the ocean of white. "I could be."

"Paint, paper, change, fix. Do whatever you want."

I wanted to go back to senior year and elope, but since that wasn't on the table . . .

"Thanks."

The same slow smile I'd dreamed of for so long rolled from the middle of his lips to the edges, and my heart did the same flip-flop it always had. Then he pounded up the stairs and disappeared through a doorway.

I uncovered pencils and a raggedy notebook in a kitchen drawer, then walked through the rooms on the first floor, taking notes, making sketches, starting a list of what I would need to undo the eye-burning décor. I'd also need to replace the god-awful furniture Gideon must have picked up on the side of the road in some college town the day after final exams ended. I could only hope he hadn't found the mattresses in the same place.

When I came up for air, I had several lists, along with sketches showing where new furniture would go and which walls I wanted to knock down.

Gideon *had* said to do whatever I wanted. Would I get the chance before he discovered my inability to give him the heir he needed so badly and booted me onto the sidewalk? *Could* he boot me onto the sidewalk? He had taken me as his luna, could he take that back?

I moved to the window. The streets were deserted; the sun fell like a great ball of fire toward the western horizon, casting orange and pink and magenta fingers along the edge of approaching night. Everyone was inside, having dinner, making dinner. Being human.

Gideon appeared in the window behind me, set his hands on my upper arms. "What's wrong?"

I couldn't help it, I leaned against his chest and shook my head. "I feel . . . unsettled." I shifted my shoulders, and in the glass, they moved separately from my bones—a wolf-shrug, my first. "Like my skin is too small."

"The moon is coming."

"But she's not full."

"That doesn't matter, Sunshine." He turned me around, cupped my cheek, then kissed me, so gentle, so sweet, so opposite of all that he was now, and yet I believed it. Because once upon a time his kiss had been what I lived for.

"We run under the full moon because we must." He brushed his fingers through my hair. "We run under any moon because we can."

"I'm going to feel like this all the time?" My voice went high as Minnie Mouse.

His gaze softened. "As the moon wanes so does the feeling. It's also harder to change as the moon grows small. We still can, it's just . . ." He lifted a shoulder. "Let me show you the territory we command to the north." He took my hand and tugged me toward the kitchen. "Run with me through our world. Everything will be all right."

Beyond the kitchen window, night hovered, and the moon called. God help me, I wanted to believe him. I wanted to believe *in* him as strongly as I once had.

"No one can see in." Gideon lost his shirt, unzipped his jeans.

I didn't care if they could. The itchy feeling had to be addressed, so I tossed my clothes on top of his and, naked, followed Gideon into the night. As the silvery glow cast over us, I felt not only the pull of a love I'd thought long dead but also the pull to change. Not because I had to but because I wanted to.

An eight-foot-high fence surrounded the backyard, beyond which loomed a seemingly never-ending parade of trees. The houses of neighbors on either side faced west and east; most of their windows did as well. Certainly if someone looked outside in the dark of the night, at this or that precise moment, they would see something unbelievable.

Who would they tell? And if anyone came knocking, I could always give them a mind push.

"When you get to the fence, all you gotta do is reach for your wolf and then jump. The sheen of the moon calls to the change."

We ran across the grass. Magic—cool and shimmering—danced along my skin as we leaped, easily clearing the hurdle, departing the civilized world on two legs and landing in the world of wolves on four.

The uncontrollable hunger of my first change was as absent as the pain. Gideon had promised it would only hurt the first time, and that promise, at least, had been fulfilled. Trust scratched harder at the edges of mistrust.

Ash had said I would become a beast ruled by my hunger, and I had been for a short time. Then Gideon's touch, his magic had taken that away. How could anyone not want to follow him anywhere?

The forest, the moon, the night, the air called to me. I reveled in that call and the freedom it brought me.

Gideon hip-checked me; I hip-checked him back. We twisted and tussled and behaved like puppies. I hadn't had this much fun since . . . the nineties.

Distracted, I didn't see him dart in close. He gave me a nip. I yipped, and he nuzzled me. Then he licked where he'd hurt, and I felt something else I hadn't since the nineties.

Lust and love all mixed together in a soup of heat and need and confusion.

I snarled, and he backed off, but the feeling, the memory, the need remained.

We ran until the trees thinned and the lights of another town flickered. The place looked just like any other that had been built in a clearing made by God or by man. Yet werewolves lived among them. I could feel it.

My wolves. My pack. My kind.

Gideon huffed through his nose, tossed his head, and I followed him some more as he showed me another town and then another. After that, we headed home.

Home. It had been a long time since I'd called a place *home* and felt that it was. The last time had been with him.

The fence loomed, and Gideon, several paces ahead of me, leaped, his body arching through moonshine. I heard him land on two feet. My muscles bunched in preparation, then a scent pierced the evergreen, and my head swung that way as the smell hit me hard, and the memory hit harder.

Gideon and I stroll through the woods that rim Lunar Lake, holding hands; brightly colored leaves skate downward all around us.

I stop, my nose wrinkling. "What's that?"

"Autumn." Gideon kicks aside a pile of damp leaves, revealing a stash of rotting walnuts. "Beauty on the outside, black rot underneath."

"Sarah?"

Gideon's voice from the other side of the fence brought me out of the past.

"If you're having a hard time changing, reach for the inner you. Think of yourself as Sarah, remember who you are, see you, feel you, *be* you."

My head spun, and I staggered. That smell was making it difficult to focus.

"Sarah!"

Gideon's voice centered me, brought me out of whatever that

had been. I leaped over the fence as a wolf and hit the ground as a woman. "Chill out."

"I—Sorry. For an instant, I thought—"

"That I'd run off? Where would I go?"

The truth of that question threw me. Where *would* I go like this?

Gideon took my hand. "You could go anywhere."

"And be a lone wolf? No thanks." I'd been alone a long time, even in a crowd. But I no longer felt lost. I didn't feel alone. I felt like the version of me I could have been, would have been, with him.

"What were you doing?"

"I smelled . . ." I glanced behind me, but all I could see was fence.

"What?"

Something. Nothing. Everything.

"Smells of the forest. They're distracting."

"It takes some getting used to."

Inside, Gideon picked up his jeans, handed me my own. His bare back gleamed; his pecs bunched. I wanted to touch them, taste them. Instead, I finished dressing then pretended to be interested in the moving boxes I never had unpacked while I sifted through my brain for a topic of conversation that didn't involve Gideon, me, Gideon and me doing things I had really missed doing.

"Shouldn't someone keep tabs on Zane?"

"Wendell's on it."

"Good." I moved to the window, peered at the moon. I could still feel the wind in my fur, the power in my legs, the magic rippling through my body, but it was fading.

Gideon's hands cupped my shoulders once more, and he pressed his lips to my hair. He was so warm, so familiar, so Gideon I closed my eyes and let the years of missing him, needing him, aching for him drift away. He was here now, and I could—

I opened my eyes and saw the truth reflected in the window glass again. I was starting to hate windows.

I tried to move away. "Let me go."

Gideon held on. "Never."

I lifted my chin to indicate our images painted in shades of gray and blue. "Why would you take someone who appears old enough to be your mother as your mate? Why would you tell everyone I'm your wife?"

I waited for him to say, *I had to; I promised*. I knew this was the case, but maybe if he said it again, I'd stop wishing, hoping secretly, foolishly for something else.

His breath cast over me, and I fought against an awareness I'd never thought I would feel again. Memories trembled at the edge of night, and I felt as if I might shatter.

"Because I love you, have always loved you, will never *stop* loving you."

This time when I shifted in his arms, he let go, and I turned, lifting my hands to gently touch his face. "That's a good reason."

ALWAYS COULD BE
A VERY LONG TIME

*B*zzz.
    Bzzz.

My eyes opened to a ceiling the shade of curdled buttermilk. That was going to have to go.

Bzzz.

I lay on a mattress that lay on a bare, scratched hardwood floor. No box spring. No headboard.

Bzzz.

No clothes.

Everything rushed back. Gideon loved me, had always loved me, would always love me. The same as I had, did, and always would love him. And now, considering what we were, *always* could be a very long time.

I needed to tell him the truth. He would get no heir from me.

I sat up. "Gideon?"

Nothing.

I roamed from the bedroom into the hall, across the landing. His office was empty.

Bzzz.

Following the sound downstairs, I uncovered my phone in the pocket of my jeans, which I'd shucked for the second time for a better reason. I snatched it up and strode into the kitchen. No Gideon there either. Huh.

Bzzz.

I had a message from Jenna. The instant I heard her speak, I knew something was wrong.

"I'm not sure I've ever called and you haven't picked up." She laughed, and I didn't like the sound of that either. "I . . ." Her breath rushed out. "I'm sure it's nothing, but . . ."

I leaned forward as if I could draw out the nothing, which I was pretty damn sure wasn't. The silence lengthened, and she sighed. "Just call me when you get this."

I tapped my phone harder than I needed to in order to return her call. The phone didn't even ring before I was dumped into voice mail.

My mom radar buzzed as loud as a hornet's nest. Something was not right.

"Mom calling back," I said after the beep, hoping she'd remind me soon, and for the thousandth time, that I didn't need to say who I was since the phone told her. Some habits born in elementary school are hard to break. "Call *me* when you get this."

Except she didn't.

I waited a half hour, tried her again. Straight to voice mail. No word from or sign of Gideon either.

I didn't know his cell number, no landline anywhere in the house, so I went old school and left a note—*Issue with Jenna. Back as soon as I can*—on the kitchen table before I climbed into my car.

Three hours later, the sun fell toward the horizon as I motored into Dane County; a half hour after that, the Madison city limits arrived with the dusk. I was still ten minutes from Jenna's apartment when she called me.

"Where have you been?" I asked at the same time she said, "I think I'm being followed."

My fingers clenched the steering wheel; I forced my voice to remain calm, though I felt anything but. "Why?"

"Maybe because my mom's a werewolf queen and my birth dad's the king."

"No one knows that but us, baby."

"You sure?"

"Yes." If I hadn't been, I would never have let her out of my sight.

"Maybe I'm imagining things."

"What things?"

"Footsteps in the hall that stop outside my apartment door for a disturbing amount of time before they move on. Scritch-scratch on the pavement behind me. Twitchy in the middle of my back."

"But you haven't actually seen anyone following you?"

"No. But I'm almost at my apartment."

"So am I. Stay on the line until I have you in sight."

"Mom."

"Humor me."

"Fine." Her breath came faster, in syncopation with a distant echo of her steps. "Okay. I'm turning onto my street."

Her steps slowed. Then they stopped.

"Uh . . . hi."

"Hi." A man. Sounded familiar.

Jenna must have put her phone into her pocket because her voice became muffled.

"Wendell, right?"

Wendell was supposed to be watching Zane. Did that mean Zane was close?

"What are you doing here?" Jenna asked.

Yeah, what?

"I'm the beta. Everything I do is for the safety of pack, it occurred to me that we would have to wait years before an heir is old enough to do battle, to keep us safe. The alpha's strong. We'll probably be all right, but . . . why take the chance when you're here and you're fully grown?"

How does he know? ran through my head.

"Run!" came out of my mouth, but my daughter couldn't hear me.

"Okay, then," Jenna said. "B-bye." She fumbled for the phone. "That guy is we—"

"Run, Jenna!" My foot went lead. "Get inside and lock the doors."

"What? He's gone."

He wasn't. I didn't know how Wendell knew Jenna was Gideon's, but he did, and he planned to act on it. Unless I stopped him.

"Listen to your mother and run!"

I turned onto her street just as the moon came over the horizon. The avenue was barren. Then a white wolf with patches of bald on his winter-starved, scrawny carcass emerged from a thick foliage lining the sidewalk.

I lifted my foot from the gas, and the car coasted to the curb.

If I hadn't known he was up to no good from his kooky-ass conversation with my daughter, I would have figured it out by his hunched back, his lifted ruff, his skulking, stalking slither.

Jenna took one look at him and bolted.

Next thing I knew I spilled from the car and into a shaft of moonlight. I reached for the wolf within, and I changed.

That strange scent of rot I'd smelled in the forest twice before swirled past my face, and I stumbled, suddenly all legs. I needed to concentrate on quadrupedal instead of bipedal—now— because Wendell was airborne, and Jenna was still fifty yards from the apartment building.

His paws hit her in the back; his weight threw her to the

ground. Her forehead hit the grass with a dull *thunk*. At least she'd missed the concrete. God only knew how.

He was on top of her, saliva dripping; the moon sparked off his fangs like a diamond in the sun. I barreled into him broadside, knocking him off my daughter. Then, with the fury of a mother whose child was in danger, I lost my shit. Using tooth and claw and tooth again, I tore and slashed and tore.

Gideon had told me that the wolf within could get out if I wanted her to, and right now . . . oh baby, I wanted her to.

We rolled, end over end. Snarls, growls, yelps ensued. We gained our feet; we thumped chests and lost those feet again. Sure, I bled, but Wendell . . .

He never stood a chance. In my brain, all I saw was him touching Jenna; in my ears, all I heard was the thrum of . . .

Slash. Tear. Bite.

Kill.

"Mom?"

The voice pierced my insanity.

"I think he's dead now."

Slowly I came back from the verge—okay, well past the verge—and got a good glimpse of the damage I'd done.

I thought he was dead too. But that smell . . . rotting walnuts, which wafted off this evil, crazed werewolf, I filed that away for later.

Jenna's gaze caught on something behind me. "What the hell are you doing here?"

I whirled, and droplets of red pattered the sidewalk.

Zane stood a few feet away. "Just passing by."

"I call bullshit on that," Jenna said.

I maneuvered so I blocked his path to her. I called *bullshit* too.

It was too coincidental for Zane to be there when Wendell was supposed to be watching *him*. Though obviously Wendell had been watching Jenna instead, leaving Zane to do whatever the hell. Had he been watching Wendell or Jenna?

Either way . . . not a fan. A growl rolled free, trilling into a vicious snarl.

Zane did not seem bothered in the least by my warning. "I'd be happy to help."

"Help?" Jenna repeated.

"That body is going to . . ." He snapped his fingers as if searching for the English, even though he was old enough by a century or three to know English better than he pretended. He pointed at said body. "Do that."

"Goddammit," Jenna muttered at the same time I saw it too.

Wendell was trying to get up. How could I possibly have thought he was dead? I knew the rules.

Only silver could kill him.

I was dizzy, I was tired, but he had to die. I bolted in his direction, meaning to do whatever it took to end this.

Wendell cringed. I didn't even feel bad about that. He'd planned to kill my daughter.

The Wendell-wolf bared his throat. A silver dagger clattered onto the concrete.

"You can *grâce à moi* later."

"You are such a pretentious ass," Jenna said.

"*Merci.*"

I lifted my face to the moon's glory and reached for my inner Sarah. Motherhood. Friendship. A bachelor's in sarcasm. Yep, that was me. Zip-zap, I became a woman.

Zane's gaze drifted over me from head to toe.

"Knock it off." Jenna stepped in front of me. "She's my mom, and you're being creepy."

He lifted his eyebrows, then one slim shoulder slid up, then down in that Gallic shrug. Was it the blood that he liked? Because it certainly couldn't be the naked body of a forty-plus-year-old menopausal woman. Most likely Zane was just being Zane. Creepy, as Jenna had pointed out.

I knelt at Wendell's side and picked up the dagger, but he seemed so pathetic. Maybe I should call Gideon before—

Wendell snarled and lunged for my throat.

"Mom!"

Wendell pretty much impaled himself. Then I learned that arterial spray explodes like a shaken can of Coke. Could have done without that lesson.

As he died, Wendell shifted into a shriveled, bony, pale old man. I glanced around, shocked that no one had come out of their homes, no one had walked around the corner. From the lack of sirens, no one had called the cops.

That was nothing less than magic.

Even though I'd seen a similar light show only a few days past, I wasn't prepared for the force of the silver flares that shot from Wendell to me, smacking between my breasts hard enough that I landed on my ass, then I couldn't get off it because those flares kept coming—whack, whack, whack—into my chest, so icy they felt hot. Icy-hot!

The bursts became one with the beat of my heart. My hair lifted and crackled around my head; blue lights sparked the air. I swore my blood was on fire, and my muscles pulsed larger and larger to the beat of my heart.

The final eruptions flew skyward—man, I hoped no one saw them. By the time my eyes quit dancing with electric neon stars, Wendell was nothing but bones and ash.

"Holy hell," Jenna whispered.

Zane kicked the pile of Wendell—he seemed to enjoy it more than he should—and the ash lifted, blowing away on a western wind. The bones remained. Strange. There'd been no bones left after Ash had shot wolf-girl. Those *Jager-Sucher* bullets really made clean ups a snap.

"Well," Zane said, by far too cheery. "Those are not going to move themselves."

"You offering to move them?" Jenna asked.

I huffed air through my nose. "Accepting a favor from Zane, probably not the best idea."

His smile widened along with my unease.

"If someone comes along and sees you covered in blood, Mom, we got a bigger problem than owing this asshole a favor."

"*Excusez-moi?*" Zane's tone was offended, but his mouth smirked, and his voice was that of the serpent in the garden.

In the distance, sirens wailed.

"We gotta go." Jenna snatched my elbow, her fingers sliding in the fresh blood as she towed me toward the apartment.

"There is still the matter of the bones."

Jenna paused, glancing heavenward before casting Zane a thoroughly exasperated glance. If I wasn't so tired, shocked, and dizzy with it, I might have worked up enough energy to be exasperated myself.

"I thought you were going to take care of them."

"*Ou Majesté*, you acknowledge that if I do this you would owe me a luna favor?"

"Never mind." Jenna marched to said bones and picked them up.

"You might not want to have human bones in your apartment, along with a naked, bloody *manman*."

Jenna juggled the bones, and a few clunked onto the concrete. When she bent to pick them up, a few more fell. It would be so much easier if they disappeared.

A wave of dizziness passed over me, and I swayed.

"What did you do?" Jenna glared at Zane, but her hands were empty.

"Not me." Zane expelled a disappointed breath. There went his luna favor. "I would have . . ." Fire shot from his fingertips and scorched the sidewalk where the bones had just been.

Well, that would certainly muck up any crime scene.

"To kill a werewolf," Zane continued, "is to take his magic, along with his life."

"What are you yammering about?" Jenna stared at her hands again as if she could make the bones reappear.

Zane stared at me, and my sluggish brain connected the dots.

"I . . . uh . . . thought how much easier it would be if they disappeared."

"Wendell's magic was to disappear things?" At least Jenna had stopped staring at the empty place the bones had been, though now she was staring at me.

I lifted one shoulder at the same time Zane said, "*Zetwal ló.*"

"English," Jenna snapped.

"Gold star."

Her mouth tightened. "Can you disappear him?"

My gaze flicked in his direction. Even before I thought just that, the widening of his smirk into a grin revealed the truth. "Inanimate objects only."

"Bummer," Jenna said. "If you knew she could get rid of the evidence on her own, why didn't you say so?"

Zane didn't bother to voice the obvious answer. What I didn't know couldn't screw up his chance to extort a favor from his queen. Court intrigue. Hey, I'd watched *The Tudors.*

Red twirling lights flickered across the sky. Our time was up.

Jenna snatched my arm, this time holding on tighter. When my knees buckled, she grabbed me around the waist with hands the shade of bloodbath and hauled me up.

"Wait," I said.

Jenna did not wait.

"My superpower."

She slowed.

My only excuse for not thinking of it sooner was . . . well, there were a lot of reasons.

"I can make him forget," I whispered.

Jenna glanced over her shoulder. "Can you do it remotely, because he's gone?"

"Fuck me."

"He wants to. Believe me."

That could be taken two ways, but the one that made the most sense was that Zane would make certain what he knew, what he'd seen would be used against me in the manner most likely to profit him.

Jenna half carried me into the building, down the hall, and into her apartment.

"Cammy?" I managed.

"Took her last exam yesterday and disappeared into the sunset." Jenna kicked open the bathroom door, turned on the shower. As soon as it was warm, she shoved me inside. "Don't come out until you've washed all the blood out of your hair."

As the water twirling down the drain was the shade of deep, dark werewolf massacre, that was going to take a while.

I stood in the shower until the just short of scalding water ran clear, then I turned the tap to cool. Gideon had said I'd run hot, and I'd laughed because I'd been running hot for months.

That wasn't funny anymore.

Instead of using my magic power to push Wendell, to make him forget what he knew about Jenna—even ask how he knew about it in the first place—I'd torn him apart, then impaled him with silver, watched his ashes float away, and disappeared his bones.

What a complete and utter shitstorm.

Gideon was in a precarious position—trying to combine two packs, one that had spent an untold amount of time letting their evil run wild. He believed he could blend these packs, increase the number of werewolves able to coexist within the world of man. He was counting on me to help him do it.

I'd been a fool to believe I might. Not only was I unable to give him the heir he needed to prove his strength, but I'd killed his beta. Which meant Gideon would have to kill me. Because the punishment for killing another wolf, outside a challenge to the alpha fought in a ring, was death.

I started to shake, not from the chill of the water but from the realization not only of what I had done but of what I would have to do.

Run.

The End

Are you ready for more of Sarah's story?
BLAME IT ON MIDNIGHT
A Midnight Madness Nightcreature Novel Book #2

BLAME IT ON MIDNIGHT

I saved my daughter. But how do I save myself?

I did what I had to. Try and kill my girl? I will end you faster than you can say *have mercy*. Sure I broke a cardinal pack rule, which will get me executed by my mate. If they find out. If they find me. And here I thought we had a second chance at love.

Saved from capture by Zane, the sexiest of sexy werewolves, my rescue comes with a price. Zane wants a favor, one that could cause an all-out pack war. The last thing I need is to make more enemies, but lives are at stake if I don't make a stand.

Not only that, but I have a secret. An impossible secret that is going to turn the entire hidden werewolf world upside down.

From the voice of *New York Times* bestselling author Lori Handeland, a new volume in her Nightcreature world, complete with the humor, depth of characterization and fast-paced plot lines she is known for while showcasing the author's incredible range.

BLAME IT ON MIDNIGHT
A Midnight Madness Nightcreature Novel Book #2

DEAR READER

Dear Reader,

I hope you are enjoying the adventures of Sarah Sullivan and my foray into paranormal women's fiction with the "Midnight Madness"trilogy, loosely connected to my popular Nightcreature Novels.

Presently, there are eleven full length novels, two novellas and three short stories in the Nightcreature world, along with another spinoff trilogy, "Sisters of the Craft." A list of all my novels can be found on my website.

When the paranormal women's fiction genre came into being several years ago, a writer friend suggested I try my hand. Other commitments kept me from doing so right away, but when I did, Sarah was right there waiting for me—an older heroine, like me, ready for love and adventure.

Word-of-mouth can really help an author out, so if you enjoyed this book, I'd love it if you shared that with your friends.

In the same vein, reviews are critically important. If you're so inclined, I'd appreciate a Review (it can be as short as you'd like) on the platform where you purchased it. I would appreciate it very much!

I love hearing from my readers and can be contacted via my website (LoriHandeland.com), through Facebook (Lori Handeland Books) and on Instagram (Lori Handeland Books).

Best Wishes,
   Lori Handeland

ABOUT THE AUTHOR

Lori Handeland is a five-time nominee and two-time winner of the prestigious RITA™ Award from Romance Writers of America, as well as the New York Times and USA Today bestselling author of over sixty novels spanning the genres of paranormal romance, urban fantasy, contemporary romance, historical romance, historical fantasy and women's fiction. Her novel *Just Once* received a coveted, starred review from Library Journal and was optioned as a feature film by Catalyst Global Media.

Lori lives in Southern Wisconsin with her husband of over thirty-five years. In between writing and reading, she enjoys long walks with their rescue mutt, Arnold, and visits from her two grown sons, awesome daughter-in-law and perfectly adorable grandchildren.

MORE BOOKS BY LORI?

I have written over sixty novels, novellas and short stories across multiple genres. But whether you read a contemporary or a historical, a women's fiction or a paranormal, you will always find my signature voice, along with a little humor, a little angst and the depth of characterization and fast-paced plot lines I love to read as well as write.

You can download a complete LIST of my novels on my website.

COPYRIGHT

Nothing Good Happens After Midnight
   Copyright © 2023 Lori Handeland
   Cover Art The Killion Group, Inc.